I0726379

STRIKEFORCE AGENT
VALERIE INGLEWOOD

ONE BAD APPLE

T.K. WILDE

Dreamstone Publishing © 2016

www.dreamstonepublishing.com

Copyright © 2016 Dreamstone Publishing and T.K. Wilde

All rights reserved.

ISBN: 1925499251

ISBN-13:   978-1-925499-25-4

Disclaimer

This is a work of fiction. Any resemblance to persons living or deceased is purely coincidental, and is not intended.

Dedication

To my readers – without you, there would be no stories.

To all of my family and friends, who support me when I am writing, and make it possible for books to get finished – thank you!

Table of Contents

Chapter 1

Charlene Brockworth elbowed Valerie Inglewood in the ribs. "Wake up, sleepy head. The day's half over."

Valerie dragged her head off the car window. She rubbed her eyes and rubbed her neck. "Where are we?"

"We just crossed the New Mexico state line." Charlene handed her a bag of pretzels. "Are you hungry?"

Valerie made a face. "Not for that. Don't you know how bad those things are for you?"

Charlene wedged the bag between her knees. "All the more for me. We'll be stopping for gas in Taos. You can get something to eat there. Can you hold out that long?"

"I can hold out as long as it takes to get something edible." Valerie rolled down her window and gazed out at the expanse of rolling countryside. "I've never been to New Mexico before."

"This part isn't much to look at," Charlene told her. "But the rest of the state is stunning. It's especially nice up in the mountains where we're going."

"Where exactly are we going?" Valerie asked.

"You didn't tell me anything when we left. You just dragged me out of the office on a moment's notice. Is that standard operating procedure for the Strikeforce Team, or is it your idea of a joke at my expense?"

Charlene chuckled. "It isn't my idea. We don't get called up until the last minute, so when we get a case, we have to leave right away. It's the nature of the beast."

"You'd think they would at least give us time to pack our things." Valerie ran her fingers through her hair and let the wind brush it out of her face. "I didn't even get to bring my toothbrush."

"When are you going to learn?" Charlene asked. "The team sends your personal things for you. You'll get them when we get there."

"That's what you always say," Valerie replied. "So far, our things have arrived after we wrapped up the case and went home. The same thing has happened on every case we've worked on."

Charlene laughed. "That's because you're such a hot-shot investigator. You have all these cases solved in a matter of days. Most people take weeks or months to solve their cases. The team can't help it if you're a whiz kid."

"Then they should at least let me pack a bag before I leave," Valerie replied. "It would save a lot of hassle."

"I'll pass that on to Colonel Tomlinson," Charlene told her. "Maybe he'll make an exception for you."

"Good," Valerie replied. "Now tell me about this case. I don't even know where we're going."

"We're going to a spiritual retreat center in the mountains north of Santa Fe," Charlene told her. "The nearest town is a little speck on the map called Tesuque. We turn off the highway there and head into the deepest, darkest mountains. That's where we'll find our case waiting for us. The place is called EdenCloud."

"EdenCloud!" Valerie repeated. "It sounds like something an eight-year-old made up."

"Maybe they think it's like the Garden of Eden," Charlene replied. "And I guess it's up in the clouds."

"No kidding," Valerie shot back. "So what's the case? What do we know about it?"

"Cold-blooded murder," Charlene replied. "A man by the name of Harold Henderson was strangled before dinner, and everybody in the place is a suspect. That's all we know."

Valerie frowned. "That's a heck of a can of worms to find at a spiritual retreat center. Wouldn't you expect the inmates to be too pure for that?"

Charlene snorted. "Inmates!"

Valerie blushed. "What am I supposed to call them—customers? Or how about campers?"

"How about residents?" Charlene replied. "Calling them inmates sounds too severe. It's not a mental hospital, you know."

Valerie gazed out the window. "Spiritual retreat center—mental hospital—what's the difference? If they're unstable enough to strangle a man to death, they're no more spiritually superior to anybody else on the planet."

Charlene munched her pretzels. "Never mind that. Stick to the case, Watson."

"What else is there?" Valerie asked. "Do we know anything about the suspects?"

"Apparently," Charlene replied, "this Harold Henderson went by the name Firehawk."

Valerie guffawed with laughter. "That's a good one."

Charlene suppressed a smile. "It's a little unusual, I grant you. But once we get up there, we're going to have to keep it strictly professional. Get your jollies out now, sweetheart, because once we pull into the driveway, I expect you to keep your cool no matter what. Do you understand me?"

Valerie cast her a sidelong glance and snickered under her breath. "Let me guess. They all have code names. Who else have we got on the roster — Dances With Guinea Pigs? What about Dandelion Puff? Or Rottweiler Breath?" She burst out laughing again. "I can't wait to get there."

Charlene shook her head. "All right. All right. Have a good laugh. I know the names are strange, but you can't fault them for trying to improve their lives. Only one of them is a killer. I'm sure the others are good people who got caught in the wrong place at the wrong time."

Valerie shrugged. "They might not be killers, but if they pay good money to run away from the world to improve their lives, they must have some serious problems. You know the old saying. A normal person is someone you don't know very well."

Charlene shot her a grin. "If that's true, you must be as crazy as they are."

"I might be," Valerie replied. "But at least I don't go locking myself away in the mountains to fix myself. I just keep on trucking."

Charlene pulled into a gas station. "Get something to eat while we're here. We've got another two hours on the highway, and who knows how long it could take us driving into the mountains before we get there? You might not get another chance."

Valerie stared at her. "Don't tell me you don't know how far away the place is."

Charlene grabbed the pump handle. "No, I don't know. On the map they gave me, the road to the place peters out after fifty miles. I don't know how far it is beyond that."

Valerie gasped. "Fifty miles! Fifty miles off the highway? But that's...."

Charlene nodded. "See what I mean? Get in there and get something to eat."

Valerie stumbled into the gas station and came back with a grocery bag loaded to the breaking point. She set it on the passenger seat floor between her feet. Charlene came back from paying for the gas and slid behind the wheel. "What did you get?"

Valerie opened her bag. "I got some fruit and some nuts and some beef jerky and some roasted chicken legs. Do you want some?"

Charlene made a face. "Haven't you got anything with sugar?"

Valerie grabbed a bag of nuts and started crunching. "They probably won't have Twinkies and HoHos up at the center."

"No, they won't," Charlene replied. "They're hard core vegetarians."

"Hmm," Valerie muttered. "Maybe I should bring a whole roast chicken."

Charlene fired up the engine, and they drove on south through the desert. The highway wound through the foothills and through rambling towns until Charlene turned off at a deserted country store. "This is it."

Valerie looked around. "What is?"

"This is Tesuque," she replied. "This is where the blacktop ends."

Charlene dropped into low gear, and they started up a gravel road winding into the mountains. Valerie stared in wonder as the store disappeared. Everything disappeared except pine trees, scrubby bushes, and the powdery red earth under their tires.

Valerie swallowed hard and took a comforting drink from her water bottle. What if they got lost out here in the mountains and no one knew where they were? What if Firehawk's killer tried to kill them, too? This EdenCloud place probably wouldn't have cellular coverage. They might not even have the internet. Then what would she do? How could she and Charlene solve their case without basic contact with the outside world?

Clouds of orange dust billowed up from the car wheels and blocked her view of the surroundings. She had no choice but to lose herself in her own thoughts. And her thoughts invariably turned on the worst possible scenario in front of her. Who was this Firehawk? What would make a man change his name from something sensible like Harold Henderson to Firehawk? You couldn't come up with a more ridiculous situation if you tried. And now he was dead. His fellow inmates, now suspects in his murder, must be as wacky as he was.

All of a sudden, Charlene leaned on the brakes. She skidded to a stop, and clouds of dust filled the car. Valerie choked and coughed. "What's going on? Did the car die?" That was the last thing they needed right now.

"Look." Charlene pointed to a tree by the side of the road.

Valerie waved the dust away, but just as much dust surrounded them outside the car as inside. She squinted through the murk and could just make out a sign tacked to the tree. "EdenCloud. That's odd. What's that doing there?"

Charlene shook her head and threw the car into gear again. "They didn't say anything about another turn-off. Maybe someone didn't want us to find the place."

Then Valerie noticed another dirt road—more like a narrow trail—plunging down a ravine into the trees. "We're not going down there, are we?"

Charlene shifted into reverse and backed up. "What do you suggest? That we go back to Denver and tell Colonel Tomlinson that someone gave us the wrong directions so we bagged the whole case? The center must be down there, and we're going in."

Valerie gulped, and the car rolled over the edge of the cliff. She gripped the door handle until her fingers ached, but Charlene kept a firm hold on the steering wheel and her foot jammed on the brake. They plummeted down the slope, and Valerie left her last shred of hope on the top road behind them.

Chapter 2

Down and down they went until the road flattened out and wound through more trackless forests. At last, it emerged into a sunny field of wildflowers, surrounded on all sides by dense pine forests. The blue sky was a vast vault overhead. The dust cloud from the car's tires sailed out behind them, and Valerie got a good look at the landscape. "It's not so bad down here."

"Not so bad!" Charlene exclaimed. "It's beautiful. I can understand why they come here for spiritual renewal—or whatever they come here for."

The car rumbled through the field. Only on the other side did they catch sight of an enormous structure jutting into the sky. Its black steel roof towered over the trees, and its sheer glass windows reflected the sun. "But this is ultra-modern. I thought they'd be living in adobe huts with pit toilets."

"It doesn't look like it." Charlene turned off the dusty track onto a flawless concrete driveway that swept up to the building. "It doesn't look like they're short of cash at all."

Charlene parked in the parking lot between three BMWs and a couple of Jaguars. She set the hand brake and propped the door open. "You better leave you chicken legs in the car until we find out what their food policy is."

"I'm sure they won't mind me putting them in the fridge," Valerie replied.

Charlene shrugged. "Just leave them here until we know for certain."

Valerie gazed up at the building. Charlene rubbed the cuff of her sleeve against the windshield. A crust of dust-smudged her shirt, but the car looked just the same. Valerie couldn't see into the car through the thick coat of dust.

The two women strode up the curved steps to the front entrance. Massive glass doors opened into a high-ceilinged hall with palm trees growing in open beds in the middle of it. Their fronds raked the blue ether above Valerie's head. Charlene looked around. "Where's the reception desk?"

"No reception desk." The voice made them jump. They whirled around and found themselves face to face with a bald woman in a bright yellow robe. "You must be the investigators."

Charlene stuck out her hand. "I'm Charlene Brockworth, and this is Valerie Inglewood. We got here as soon as we could."

"I'm Sri Danke," the woman replied. "You are welcome to our humble retreat."

Charlene bit her lip. "Sri Danke? That's not your real name, is it?"

The woman stiffened, and her smile vanished. "It is my real name. It is as real as any other name I have ever used."

"But it isn't the name you were given at birth, is it?" Charlene asked.

"No, it isn't," Sri Danke replied. "My parents gave me a name of their own choosing, but as a free individual in the spirit world, I chose to christen myself with a name that means so much more."

"I suppose most of your fellow free individuals in the spirit world have done the same thing," Charlene remarked.

"Quite true," Sri Danke replied. "We use our naming ceremony to mark our evolution between bondage to the material slavery of society and the spiritual freedom of heaven."

Charlene nodded. "I understand. Now would you mind telling me what your name was before you changed it to Sri Danke?"

The woman glared at her. Her expression didn't match her shaved head and crisp, bright robe. "I could tell you, but I won't. You may call me Sri Danke. That is the only name you need to know."

Charlene pursed her lips. "I don't mean to be rude since we just met, but I'll have to remind you that we're federal agents, and we're here to investigate the murder of one of your spirit friends. The information I received says everyone here is a suspect, so if you expect me to clear your name, you'll have to tell me what it is, and everyone else will have to do the same thing. The longer you hold back on telling me that, or any other information I need to know, the more guilty you'll make yourself look. Is that understood?"

Sri Danke's expression changed from dangerous to ferocious. Then, all of a sudden, she wilted before their eyes. "All right. My original name is Barbara McGregor."

Charlene did her best not to crow in triumph. "Thank you. Now, would you mind giving us some information about..... about the man who died?"

Sri Danke pulled herself up again. "His name was Firehawk. You're free to call him whatever you want, but that was his name — that was his *real* name."

Charlene held up her hands. "I won't argue with you. We just need to know your original names for our investigation. You can call yourselves whatever you want up here, but we need to look into your lives before you came up here. One of you might have had a connection with... with the victim that connects back to his murder."

Sri Danke shrugged. "None of that matters. All that matters is that we're here, and we are free. Nothing can take that away from us."

"No one wants to take it away from you," Charlene insisted. "But a man is dead. You being free doesn't change that. Now could you please tell us what you know about his death?"

"I don't know anything," Sri Danke snapped. "I was nowhere near him when he died."

"Where were you?" Valerie asked. "What were you doing at the time of his death."

"I was in my office," Sri Danke replied. "I was on the phone with the Santa Fe City Council."

Valerie looked around in disbelief. "But surely this place is far enough away from any town to be of no concern to the City Council."

Sri Danke waved her hand. "Those fools insist on recording us in their little black books. They can't stand the idea of anyone getting free from their slave system. They want to tax us for land use and environmental degradation."

"How awful!" Charlene exclaimed. "Do you pay other taxes, or are you tax exempt?"

Sri Danke narrowed her eyes. "Just exactly what are you insinuating? Of course we pay taxes. We aren't criminals, you know."

"They must think this building makes an impact on the environment," Valerie pointed out. "I can understand why they might think so. You have a septic system and electric lights and an air conditioning system, don't you?"

"This building doesn't make anywhere near as much impact on the environment as their filthy city," Sri Danke returned.

"We use solar power for all our electricity, and we use a special worm composting system instead of a septic tank for our wastes. We grow all our own food, and we leave nothing behind. We're the most innovative, environmentally conscious business in the state."

Charlene sighed. "Okay. Could we get back to the murder? So you were in your office on the phone with the City Council - were you alone?"

"Of course I was alone," Sri Danke replied. "I couldn't exactly talk on the phone with a bunch of people around, could I?"

"So how did you hear about Firehawk?" Charlene asked.

"Eagle Feather rushed into the office and told me," Sri Danke replied. "I had to excuse myself in the middle of the phone call. It was extremely annoying, I can tell you."

Charlene smiled. "I'll bet it was. Did you go see the body then?"

Sri Danke nodded. "He was lying right outside the kitchen door."

"What did he look like?" Valerie asked.

"What did he look like?" Sri Danke repeated. "He looked dead. That's what he looked like. He was ash white, and his skin hung off his bones. He looked like a lump of dead flesh. You could see the bright red finger marks around his throat where someone choked him."

"I'm sorry for your loss," Charlene told her. "You must have been traumatized by the sight."

"The souls rostered to set the table for dinner had to step over his mortal shell to get from the kitchen to the table," Sri Danke went on. "We would have canceled dinner, but all the other souls were standing around waiting to eat. We couldn't exactly send them to bed hungry, now could we?"

"So that's what you call yourselves," Valerie remarked. "You call yourselves souls. We wondered...." Valerie stopped talking when she saw the expression on Charlene's face. "Did you think about calling the police?"

Sri Danke stared at her. "The police? The Santa Fe Police? You must be joking."

"Why?" Valerie asked.

"You've got a dead man in your dining room with the visible marks of strangulation around his throat. I would think your first reaction would be to call the police."

"No, no, no, no, no." Sri Danke flapped her hands.

"We would never call the Santa Fe Police over anything, especially not something as sensitive as this. We're free individuals in the spirit world. The police are the enforcers of the slave mentality. They could never understand us well enough to respect our dignity or the sanctity of our environment. They already think we're deranged. This would only make matters worse."

Charlene nodded. "I see. Well, we're here, so we'll find out who killed him. Do you know if he had any enemies around the center?"

"Firehawk never had any enemies, around the center or anywhere else," Sri Danke replied. "He was the most spiritually evolved soul among us. He used to sit under a tree for days at a time and eat nothing but brown rice. All the other souls at EdenCloud would bow down before him and ask his advice. He was a font of wisdom and universal love."

Charlene and Valerie exchanged glances. "He sounds like the kind of person people love until they start hating them."

"No one hated Firehawk," Sri Danke told her. "Everybody loved him."

"If he was sitting under a tree, what was he doing in the dining room outside the kitchen door?" Valerie asked. "Did he plan to come to the dining room and eat with everybody else, or was that a surprise to you?"

"I don't know what his plans were," Sri Danke replied. "He came and went as he pleased. He had been under a tree for a week, right up until the day he died, but he could have decided to come into dinner that day. I really don't know."

"When was the last time you spoke to him?" Charlene asked. "Did you bow before him on a regular basis?"

Sri Danke narrowed her eyes at the tall investigator. "I am a free individual. I do not bow before anybody, no matter how wise they might be. I hadn't spoken to Firehawk in a week. I hadn't even seen him since he went outside. I'm far too busy running this center. I didn't see him anywhere except in the dining room when he came there to eat."

"So you run the center," Valerie remarked. "I suppose somebody has to do it. Not everybody can be a free individual in the spirit world."

"I am a free individual in the spirit world," Sri Danke shot back. "Running the center doesn't change that."

"I meant somebody has to get their hands dirty paying taxes and fighting off the city council," Valerie explained.

"Somebody has to deal with the enforcers of the slave mentality. How did you wind up with the job?"

"I started EdenCloud," Sri Danke waved her hand to one side.

"Everything you see here is my handiwork. I carry the burden of running the center so the other souls can get on with their work of elevating their souls to heaven. That is my role here, and I embrace it with love and grace."

Valerie's eyes widened.

"You started EdenCloud? Then you must know everything there is to know about its finances. You must know more than anybody about the people who come here to use your services."

"That's right," Sri Danke replied.

"Then you'll be the one we'll talk to about your..... what do you call 'ems?" Valerie glanced at Charlene.

"We're calling them residents." Charlene turned to Sri Danke. "Is that okay with you?"

Sri Danke shrugged. "We call them souls, but you may call them residents."

"Good." Charlene turned away. "Now, if you show us where we're going to stay, we'll get settled in before we start our investigation."

Sri Danke stared at her. "Where you're going to stay? What are you talking about?"

"Well, we have to stay somewhere, don't we?" Charlene replied.

"But you're not staying here," Sri Danke told her.

"You're here to investigate Firehawk's death, not to stay. I spoke to Colonel Tomlinson on the phone myself, and he never said anything about staying."

"Well, we can't exactly investigate his death without staying here, can we?" Charlene pointed out.

"It's three o'clock in the afternoon. We won't have the case wrapped up in two hours, and we sure as shootin' aren't going to drive down to Santa Fe and stay in a hotel room each night. I don't care what you say. I'm not driving up and down that hill until we wrap up the case and arrest Firehawk's murderer. We're staying here in the meantime, and you're going to find somewhere to put us up."

Charlene crossed her arms over her chest. Sri Danke stared at her in a wordless turmoil of emotion. Then she threw up her hands. "Oh, all right. If that's the way you want it, all right."

Chapter 3

Sri Danke spun on her heel and stomped off. She vanished into a side door and came back with an enormous key chain. She didn't look at the investigators but headed down a hall to one side. She hadn't gone more than a few steps, though, when the front entrance door burst open and a tall man with sandy brown hair charged into the building. He wore plain blue jeans and a cotton shirt buttoned up the front. Clean brown cowboy boots showed under the cuffs of his jeans.

"Where is he?" he bellowed. "Where is he, you freaks?"

Sri Danke spun back around the other way. "How dare you? This is private property, and you are trespassing. I'll ask you to leave immediately."

The man spotted her orange robe and strode toward her with his eyes blazing. "Are you the nut in charge around here? If you are, you're the person I'm looking for. I'm Dan Henderson, and I'm here to get my father's body. I went to the police morgue in town, and they said they didn't know anything about it. When I told them my father died up here, they said they hadn't even had a report of a death up here, and if it was true, his body would be here. So where is he? I'm taking his body back to Phoenix for a decent burial."

Sri Danke opened her mouth, but the man cut her off.

"Don't tell me you subjected my father's remains to any of your wacko New Age cult rituals. Don't tell me you buried him up here. I don't care what cockamamie nonsense you preached while he was alive, but he's not gonna be buried up here, not as long as I've got breath in my body to stop it."

Sri Danke got over her surprise. "We did not bury Firehawk. We...."

Dan held up a hand to silence her. "Don't use that stupid phony name. Call him by his real name or don't talk about him at all."

Sri Danke hesitated.

"As I was about to say, we did not bury.... your father. We had to wait until these federal agents arrived to investigate the case."

Dan paused and scrutinized Charlene and Valerie.

"Federal agents?"

Charlene extended her hand. "I'm Charlene Brockworth. Please accept my sincere condolences on the loss of your father."

He shook her hand with narrowed eyes.

"Thank you."

"This is Valerie Inglewood," Charlene told him.

Dan shook Valerie's hand, and his warm fingers closed over her hand. A sizzle of excitement shot up her arm. "Nice to meet you."

"We just drove in a few minutes ago, and we were interviewing..... this lady about your father's death," Charlene went on.

"We didn't know his body was still here, and we didn't know his family would be coming to collect it. We'll do our best to expedite our investigation so you can take your father home."

Dan let out a long shaky breath.

"I appreciate that, but now that you're here, I would appreciate you doing as thorough an investigation as you can. I want to know which of these freaks killed him and why."

Charlene held up her hand.

"We'll do our best for your sake, and for his, but I would appreciate it if you wouldn't use that derogatory language about the residents. I have to admit I don't agree with everything they do up here, either, but we have to keep this investigation professional. I would appreciate you doing everything you can to keep it that way."

Dan nodded.

"I understand, but it's asking a lot. These.... I mean, these people.... they poisoned my father with a bunch of idiotic nonsense about freedom and spirituality. They cost him hundreds of thousands, if not millions, of dollars and alienated him from his whole family. And now he's dead because of them. He lost everything to their rotten center, to the point that he didn't have a red penny to leave behind to me and my sisters. You have to forgive me for hating them."

Charlene opened her mouth to say something, but his words tumbled out in a rush.

"It's not the money I mind. I don't care that he left me without an inheritance. It's the lost years that burn me up. First he tried to convert us and get us to come up to this cult freak show - sorry, I can't help it. Then, when he couldn't convince us, he turned his back on us. Every time anybody tried to talk sense into him and show how these people were manipulating him out of his hard-earned money, he would fly into a rage and run back here to this.... this insane asylum. And now he's dead. I didn't even have a chance to say good-bye to him."

Valerie swallowed the lump in her throat, but she didn't trust herself to go to him. If she tried to comfort him, Charlene would accuse her of making eyes at another man when she should have been concentrating on the job.

As it was, Charlene went to him herself and put her hand on his arm.

"I understand. I really do, and we're going to find out who killed your father." She glanced at Sri Danke, who still stood still with her keys in her hand. "I don't suppose you're staying here."

Sri Danke started to reply, but Dan interrupted. "You bet your boots I'm staying here. I'm not leaving until this investigation is over. I don't care if it takes ten years. I'm staying right here until I get some answers."

"But you can't *all* stay here," Sri Danke cried. "We don't have the...."

Charlene broke in. "Don't you think you owe it to this man to let him stay on until he finds out what happened to his father? What harm can it do?"

Sri Danke's mouth gaped open and her eyes filmed over with tears. "But we come up here to get away from..... from all worldly contamination. We come up here to immerse ourselves in the clean air of heaven. We can't have people like.... like you running around. It would ruin everything."

Dan bristled, but Valerie spoke up.

"One of your free souls killed a man in the clean air of heaven. If you impede our investigation, the authorities will shut you down completely until they find out who killed him and why. I suggest you cooperate with our investigation, and that means finding a place for us to stay until we complete it. Under the circumstances, I believe finding a place for this man to stay is the right thing to do. It's what a free individual in the spirit world would do."

Sri Danke opened her mouth and shut it again. She glanced from one face to the next. At last, her shoulders sagged in defeat.

"Oh, all right. I suppose I have no choice. Follow me." She strode away down the hall.

Charlene set off after her, and Valerie started after Charlene, but she stopped when she noticed Dan hold back.

"You'd better come with us. They'll probably try to separate us. If we stick together, we can handle them better."

His face brightened, and Valerie smiled.

He really was handsome under all that rage and disappointment. Then again, he had a right to be angry after what he'd been through. He fell in at her side, and they caught up with Charlene and Sri Danke.

Sri Danke led them down the hall, away from the vaulted ceilings and palm trees in the entrance foyer. The farther they went, the farther the high glass fell behind them until the hall became dark and windowless. Only a fragment of light from the distant foyer penetrated that gloomy passage.

Doors studded the hall on either side, but not even a single framed picture or potted plant decorated the hall to brighten the place. Valerie cringed at the sound of their footfalls echoing on the bare tile floor. The place reminded her more and more of a prison or.... did she dare let herself think the words? It reminded her of a mental hospital. She shivered when Sri Danke stopped and rattled her keys.

As she slid a key into one of the locks, the sound set Valerie's nerves on edge. What horrors lay behind that door? No wonder Harold Henderson's family couldn't stand the idea of him coming to EdenCloud. Valerie would have done anything to stop someone she loved from living in a place like this.

The door swung back, and Dan, Valerie, and Charlene held their breath. Sri Danke stepped back to reveal a windowless cell with a bare metal cot in one corner, a bare toilet bowl set into the wall, a bare porcelain sink, and a glaring fluorescent light on the ceiling overhead. The three strangers stared in horror at what they saw.

"But this is just like a prison cell," Valerie cried. "We can't stay in there."

Sri Danke squared her shoulders.

"I'll have you know every soul in this place stays in a room just like this, including me. If it's good enough for us, it's good enough for you. You want to stay, and this is the only kind of room we have. You can stay here, or you can stay somewhere else. It's up to you."

They stared at the room again. They couldn't stay in there. They wouldn't. Who in their right mind would voluntarily subject themselves to that kind of treatment? Who in their right mind would come up with the idea of putting people into cells like this, and then have the audacity to claim that they were free individuals in the spirit world? The whole situation would have been hilarious if it wasn't so creepy. But under the circumstances, what could they do? They couldn't stay here and they couldn't leave.

Charlene shifted from one foot to the other.

"I suppose we could, just for a little while. We won't be in here much. We'll be walking around investigating the murder most of the time. We can come back here to sleep, and that's about it." She took a step forward.

"Once you go in, you won't come out," Sri Danke told her. "The doors lock automatically when they close. They'll open again for meals, but other than that, you'll stay in here."

Charlene whipped around. "Are you telling me that you keep your.... your inmates, locked up in their rooms all the time?"

"Not all the time," Sri Danke corrected her.

"They come out for meals and for required work periods twice a day. Other than that, they stay in their rooms for meditation and reflection. That's the way it works."

Charlene backed away.

"I'm not staying in there."

Valerie's mind whirled. She stepped forward. "Wait a minute. I have an idea."

She pulled off one of her shoes and wedged it under the door. Then she stood back and took Sri Danke's hand off the knob. The door slid a few inches and stuck. It stood open by itself. Valerie faced her friends. "We can prop the doors open so we can come and go as we please. We'll come back here to sleep at night, but the rest of the time, we'll spend out in the center, interviewing the suspects and solving the case. How does that sound?"

Charlene hesitated.

Sri Danke went to the next door down the hall and opened it, too. "One of you can stay in here."

Valerie wedged that door open with her other shoe. She followed Sri Danke to the third and final door. "How are you going to keep this door open? You don't have any more shoes."

Valerie tugged off her jacket and jammed it under the door. It held fast.

"There. Now we all have a place to sleep tonight."

Charlene let out a ragged sigh. Then she rounded on Sri Danke. "And if anyone of these doors magically happens to close and lock during the night, you and everybody else in this crazy asylum will be under arrest for kidnapping a federal agent, obstruction of justice, abetting a murderer, and conspiracy, and...." She ticked off the charges on her fingers.

Valerie laid her hand on Sri Danke's arm. "I think we can trust our friend Sri Danke to ensure that nothing like that happens. Am I right?"

Sri Danke dropped her eyes to the floor and nodded.

"Good," Valerie exclaimed. "Now, could you please show me how to connect my computer to the internet? I need to make a connection to the federal database so I can start researching the case."

Sri Danke's head shot up. "We don't have the internet here."

Valerie pursed her lips and crossed her arms over her chest. "I'm gonna lose my patience with you pretty soon. You might not let your inmates have access to the internet, but you couldn't run a business without it." She waved her hand at the building. "I won't even bother to ask how much money you make in a single season, but I can see by this building that you turn a pretty good profit. Do you really expect me to believe that you don't have electronic payments into your bank account? Do you really expect me to believe you don't have a website, and a PayPal account, and newsletters going out to all your members telling them when you're running your spiritual improvement programs? Come on! Of course you have the internet."

Sri Danke glanced from one face to the other. Then she dropped her eyes again.

"All right. I have a modem in my office. You can hook up in there."

Valerie threw back her shoulders in triumph.

"Good. And don't waste my time with that nonsense again. If I ask you a question, just answer it without making me threaten you. Okay?"

Sri Danke didn't answer. She jangled her key chain and shuffled down the hall toward the foyer. Valerie stole a glance at Dan and found him looking at her and grinning from ear to ear. Even Charlene bit back laughter.

Chapter 4

The three of them followed Sri Danke back to the entrance foyer. She led the investigators to the side door and into a very modern office with three computer screens facing the leather padded chair behind the desk. Valerie didn't miss a beat. She set her computer on the desk next to the others and opened it.

As soon as it came on, it popped up a message - *Wireless network within range.* Valerie's eyes widened. "A wireless network? I thought you said you didn't have the internet."

Sri Danke blushed.

"Well, the other souls don't need to know that. They come here to get away from all that. Only the administrators need to access the internet."

"Administrators?" Valerie repeated. "You mean there's more than one?"

"I couldn't run this place by myself," Sri Danke explained. "It's a multimillion-dollar operation."

"I guessed that," Valerie replied, "but I thought you were the head honcho."

"I am," Sri Danke told her.

"So who are the other administrators?" Valerie asked.

"There's Butterfly Wing," Sri Danke replied. "There's Featherbright, and there's AngelPie."

Valerie stared at her. "AngelPie?"

Sri Danke frowned. "What's wrong with that?"

Valerie repressed an almost overwhelming urge to snicker.

"Nothing, nothing at all. I'll have to interview all three of them. Where can I find them?"

"They'll be in their rooms right now," Sri Danke replied. "But they'll be out for dinner in a few hours. You can talk to them then."

Valerie snorted. "How convenient that the people responsible for running this operation are all under lock and key when the authorities come to question them."

"I told you...." Sri Danke began.

Valerie held up her hand for silence. "Don't waste your breath explaining any of this. It's too wacky to make sense. Just tell me one thing."

"What?" Sri Danke asked.

"Did Firehawk have anything to do with running EdenCloud?" Valerie asked. "Did he have any administration duties?"

"No," Sri Danke replied. "He never took any hand in running this place. He was too selfish."

"You said before he was the most advanced soul among you," Valerie pointed out. "What happened to that?"

"I mean," Sri Danke explained, "he was too busy with his own spiritual development, and he had the other souls eating out of his hand. He didn't have to sully himself with day to day business the way we did."

Valerie turned away. "Thanks. That will be all for now."

Sri Danke hesitated. "What do you mean?"

"You can go now," Valerie replied. "My partner and I will do some basic research on your operation and the backgrounds of those people whose real names we know. Once we have a basic understanding of the case, we'll be ready to interview your people. You can go now. We'll let you know if we need anything else."

Sri Danke glanced around. "But I can't leave you here alone. This is my private office. You might break into my computer and access confidential files."

Valerie faced her. "Listen, lady. You're under investigation for capital murder. Can you come down from the heights of spiritual ecstasy long enough to understand what that means? If you withhold any information you have on this case, you'll be in big trouble. If you know what's good for you, you'll open up your confidential files to us of your own free will. If you don't, we can email down to the courthouse in Santa Fe and get a warrant to search them anyway. Make it easy on yourself and go to your room. Meditate or do whatever you have to do and leave us to work in peace."

Valerie turned her back on Sri Danke and opened her web browser. Sri Danke hesitated another moment. Then her footsteps retreated down the hall, and a blessed silence descended over the office.

Charlene stepped into the room and clapped Valerie on the back. "Well done, Champ. I couldn't have done better myself."

Valerie made a face.

"I can see that these people need a firm hand. They aren't going to give an inch without kicking and screaming all the way. We're going to have to stand firm."

Dan stuck his head through the door. "I'd better leave you ladies to your work. I sure wish I could help you in some way, though."

"Actually," Valerie told him, "I think you should stick with us. After the way she acted in the hall when she told us the doors automatically close and lock, I think the three of us should stick together at all costs. We could be in danger up here if one of us goes off alone. These wack-jobs could resort to any kind of violence to stop us poking our noses into their business."

"I hate to admit it," Charlene replied, "but I agree with Valerie. At first, I thought these people were harmless hippies who wore too much Patchouli. Now I can see that they're a sophisticated cult with a lot of money at stake. Stick close to us, Dan. If you went off by yourself, you could be the next victim."

He nodded and sighed.

"I didn't like to say so, but I feel the same way. I can see that you two know your business. I'll stick with you, and hopefully we can work together to solve this murder."

"Take a look at this." Valerie turned her computer around so the others could see it.

"It's the federal case file on EdenCloud. They've been investigated seven times — seven times! — for racketeering, money laundering, fraud, kidnapping, insider trading, the works! So much for the clear air of heaven. These people are as crooked as they come. And can you guess who's been implicated as the ring-leader of these crimes?"

"Let me guess," Charlene offered. "It was a certain lady by the name of Barbara McGregor."

Valerie frowned.

"Hey, take a look at this here. It says that the reporting party was Harold Henderson."

The two investigators looked up at Dan. He stared back at them.

"Is that true, Dan?" Charlene asked. "Did your father report EdenCloud and its executives for criminal behavior?"

Dan gulped.

"This is the first I've heard of it. He never said anything to me, except to tell me what a beautiful place it was, how superior the people were, and how his life was never so complete before he came up here. God, he used to drive me around the bend with that talk."

Valerie typed away at her computer.

"We'll have to do some more digging to find out the truth. It's an interesting angle, though. What if your father found out the truth about EdenCloud and tried to stop it? That would be a good enough reason for them to kill him."

At that moment, a deafening siren rang through the building. The sound of a thousand locks unlocking echoed through the halls, and dozens of bald, golden-robed people filed out of the rooms on either side. The three stared in wonder as the inmates formed neat ranks, and paraded down the halls in perfect order, without saying a single word to each other. They didn't even raise their eyes from the floor.

"It must be dinner time," Valerie remarked. "We'd better go along if we want to get something to eat."

They followed the inmates, who really did start to look like prisoners in a chow line. They marched without a word into a giant room with fluorescent lights blazing overhead.

Valerie looked around. "It looks like a high school gymnasium."

Dan growled under his breath. "It looks like a slaughter house. These poor fools look like their going to their own funerals."

He was right. The light of human recognition didn't shine out of a single face. None of the inmates so much as glanced in the direction of the strangers, not even to frown. Valerie shuddered.

"Did you know it was like this? Did you know your father got mixed up in this?"

"I didn't know it was as bad as this," Dan replied. "But I could tell by the way he acted that it was pretty bad. The first time he came back to Phoenix from here, he used to wake up screaming in the middle of the night." Dan shook his head sadly.

"During the day, he would fill our heads with a bunch of nonsense about how wonderful it all was, but when I held him, shaking and sweating, after waking up from those nightmares, I knew it wasn't true. That's when I made up my mind to stop him. It didn't work, though. If I find out I did anything that lead to his death, I'll never forgive myself."

Charlene laid her hand on his shoulder. "You did everything you could, and you're doing more now than anyone could ask you to. You'll get justice for your father. I promise you that."

"Thanks," he muttered.

They took their places at the end of the line and copied the inmates by taking their stainless steel trays to the front counter. Not until they got to the front of the line did they see what kind of food the kitchen crew deposited on each tray. Four robed characters stood behind the counter with their eyes downcast. They dumped heaps of unidentifiable slop into the compartments of each tray.

Valerie stared down at the stuff with a sinking heart, but she got swept along with the crowd until she sat on a bench at the long table between Dan and Charlene. "What is this stuff?"

"Who knows?" Dan murmured. "What I wouldn't give right now for a nice rare steak."

Valerie looked up into his eyes, and her heart soared. Here at last was a kindred spirit. Maybe they could run off together to a restaurant in Santa Fe and get themselves some real food. How were they supposed to get through the night on this stuff?

At that moment, a man spoke up from the other side of the table. "The yellow one is dahl, and the brown one is hummus. The green one is spinach."

Sri Danke sat at his side, and she nodded in agreement. "This is Butterfly Wing. You said you wanted to talk to him. Now you can."

Valerie squinted at her tray. "I can't tell which one is yellow and which one is green. How can you tell?"

Charlene took up a forkful of one of the items. She examined it at close range, but she didn't put it in her mouth. "We heard you were vegetarians."

"We're much more than vegetarians," Butterfly Wing informed her. "We're vegans."

Valerie paused. Then she summoned all her courage. "But we thought you must have chickens for eggs and cows for milk."

"We don't eat eggs or milk," Butterfly Wing replied. "That would be unethical. We don't exploit animals in any way."

"Then how do you get protein?" Valerie asked. "The human body wasn't designed to function on dahl and hummus and spinach."

Butterfly Wing turned away.

"The human body might not have been, but the human spirit thrives on a diet pure and untainted by the life blood of any other living thing."

"What about the plants?" Valerie asked. "The spinach is a living thing. You're consuming the life blood of that."

Charlene cut her off with a wave of her hand. "Never mind. You can eat anything you want, and we'll eat the same thing while we're here. We have more important things to talk about than the food."

She still didn't put the food into her mouth. Dan didn't even touch it.

"We want to talk to you, Butterfly Wing," Charlene went on, "about your position as an administrator of EdenCloud. Is this a good time to talk?"

Butterfly Wing glanced at Sri Danke, but she kept her eyes fixed on her tray.

Valerie spoke up. "Would you mind telling me your real.... I mean, what your name was before you came to EdenCloud? It would help us to clear you of any wrongdoing."

His face brightened. "It was Charles Farnsworth."

Charlene cleared her throat. "Thank you, Now would you mind telling us about your administrative duties here at the center?"

He stirred his dahl. "I keep the books, and I keep track of bookings and attendance."

"Oh, good!" Charlene exclaimed. "Then you can fill us in on the investigations underway against EdenCloud for financial indiscretions. Do you know the details of those?"

His eyes skipped over to Sri Danke again, but she didn't offer him any help. "I know about them."

"We just looked up the details on the federal database," Valerie put in. "I didn't see your name mentioned."

"That's because I only took over my position six months ago," Butterfly Wing replied. "Someone else handled the position before that."

"Who?" Valerie asked.

No one said a word.

"It wasn't Firehawk, was it?" Valerie asked.

Sri Danke broke in on the conversation. "No, no. It wasn't Firehawk. It was someone else who isn't here anymore."

"Who was it?" Charlene asked.

Valerie picked up a speck of spinach on the end of her fork and studied it. How bad could it be? At least it was something green, and she couldn't exactly go without food up here. She took a deep breath and stuck it in her mouth.

Sri Danke and Butterfly Wing looked at each other and then back at their food. "It was Woodpecker."

Valerie choked on the spinach and it came out through her nostrils. She covered her mouth with her hand and coughed and gagged. She fought for breath and struggled out of her seat. She ran from the room, out of the building, and out into the parking lot with spinach sticking to her face.

Chapter 5

As soon as she got out into the open air, Valerie doubled over with laughter and coughed the rest of the hideous stuff out of her mouth. Then she collapsed on the ground in hysterics. "Woodpecker!"

She would have run all the way back to Denver then and there, but one thought stopped her. She went over to Charlene's car and got her grocery bag off the floor. She popped the back door and sat on the bumper in the shade. She pulled out her carton of chicken legs and started gnawing.

The sound of footsteps brought her head around in a hurry. "Do you mind if I join you?"

Valerie smiled at Dan and moved over to make room for him. She passed him the carton. "Help yourself. It could be your last meal for a month."

He pulled the meat off the bones with his teeth. "I should have known a girl like you would have a stash somewhere."

Valerie chuckled. "I would have brought the whole bloomin' chicken coop if I'd known the food was going to be like this. I don't know how long I can hold out with the food I've got."

"At least we've still got gas in our cars," he pointed out. "We can always make a run for it if we get too desperate."

"Stick close, Tonto," Valerie replied. "We're in enemy territory here."

Dan laughed and took another leg. "So what's a nice girl like you doing in a cesspit like this?"

"I'm just a federal agent investigating a murder case," she replied. "I'm innocent, I swear it."

Dan shook his head. "These people are the worst. They can rope in the most well-meaning person and take them for all they're worth. If they can do it to my dad, they can do it to anybody."

"What was he like?" Valerie asked. "We know almost nothing about him."

"He was a savvy businessman," Dan replied. "He could see through any scam. I still can't figure out how they got him hooked on their airy-fairy nonsense."

"We should take a closer look at their recruiting practices," Valerie told him. "They've been investigated for kidnapping. Some of these cults grab people right off the street. They keep them locked up and starved and tortured until they join. They fear for their lives, and that's what keeps them in."

Dan shook his head. "If they did that to my dad, I'll kill every last mother's son of 'em. I swear to God, I won't rest until the suckers are dead."

Valerie touched his arm. "Take it easy. We don't know that's what happened. Just keep your shirt on until we know the truth."

At that moment, a man walked up to them, and Valerie and Dan stared at him in disbelief. His brown hair hung down around his ears, and he wore shorts and a brown T-shirt with the Fed Ex logo on the lapel. He strode up to the car with an envelope in one hand and a cell phone in the other. "Are you Dan Henderson?"

Dan pushed himself off the bumper. "That's me. Who wants to know?"

The man held out the envelope. "I've been driving all over creation looking for you. I went to your house in Phoenix, and they told me you went to the Santa Fe Police station. So I went there, and they told me you were here. Sign this. This envelope is for you."

Dan signed his clipboard and took the envelope. The man disappeared, back in the direction of the road in, and Dan turned the envelope over and over in his hand. "What is it?"

"Only one way to find out." He tore it open and spread out the single sheet of paper it contained.

My dear son--

If you're reading this, I'm either dead or have disappeared, never to return. I pray to God you are safe, but my own foolish activities have caught up with me. Please forgive me for lying to you all these years, but it was the only way to ensure the safety of innocent people, and even some guilty ones.

Three years ago, I attended a seminar on personal development and got swept up into an organization known as EdenCloud. I didn't know then how insidious and corrupt they were. I thought it was a harmless self-improvement system. After about a year, I started having doubts, and decided to end my involvement with them.

I wrote a letter to the administration about my decision, but the very same day, a man approached me in the shower at the gym. He told he was a federal agent working on a special investigation team known as Strikeforce. He said that they were trying to bust EdenCloud for criminal activity, and he asked if I would go undercover to get evidence for them. I agreed, and that was when I started attending seminars at the retreat center near Santa Fe.

You can confirm the truth of this by contacting Colonel Tomlinson at the Strikeforce office in Denver. No one knows but him that I went undercover, working for them. You can also contact a man named Harold Clay in Pasadena, California.

He was EdenCloud's accountant for over thirty years before he left, and he has enough evidence to convict the top administrators many times over. He's the one they called Woodpecker.

There is one more person who can help you, and that is a man by the name of Ebert Cornell. He knows more about EdenCloud than anybody except the woman who started the organization, but you might find it hard to track him down. I don't know where he lives, but his name within the organization is Snowdrop. I never met him myself, but Colonel Tomlinson told me he recruited Snowdrop to work undercover, too. Snowdrop went up to the center and then broke off all contact with the Strikeforce Team. If you can find him, you will be able to put a stop to EdenCloud once and for all.

This whole process has been harrowing and soul-destroying for me, but no part of it was as hard as breaking my ties with you, my son, and your sisters. I hope you can understand now, after I am gone, why I had to do it.

I hid my life savings in an account offshore to create the illusion that I had donated all of my money to the organization. I have included the bank account number, the password, and the SWIFT code below so that you and your sisters can retrieve your rightful inheritance.

Remember the good times we had together, my dear son, and not the horror of these last few years. Please remember that I played a role for the benefit of others. I would give anything to have spared you the heartache of seeing me throw my life away, but I could not, in good conscience, stand by and let these people ruin any more lives without doing something to stop them.

I love you more than life itself. Your loving father

Always,

Harold Henderson

Dan let the paper fall to the ground and gazed at the distant line of trees surrounding the valley. Then his shoulders began to shake with silent tears. He covered his face with his hands.

"All these years, he was undercover to bust these people. If only I had known."

Valerie hesitated. Then she put her carton of chicken legs aside and put her arm around his shoulders. He wept silently, and she hugged him against her body. What could you say to a man who'd just got a letter like that, from beyond the grave? He leaned against her for support and let himself weep.

After a while, he sat up and wiped the tears off his face with his shirt cuff. He picked up the paper and folded it into a small square. "Well, that's that. We know what we have to do. We have to find this Snowdrop. Then we can destroy this place and all its heinous malarkey."

He deposited a tear-stained kiss on the paper and tucked it into his pocket.

"Let's roll."

"Hang on." Valerie held him back with her hand on his arm.

"Not so fast. We still don't know who killed your father. Snowdrop won't be able to tell us that. We don't know if Snowdrop will testify against EdenCloud, or even where he is. He could be dead, too. Your father said Snowdrop broke off contact with Colonel Tomlinson. He could have gone over to the other side. We didn't finish interviewing Butterfly Wing, and we still have two more administrators to interview. We've got lots of work to do yet."

Dan stood up.

"And we'll have to contact this Strikeforce Team. They'll be able to help us crack this case."

Valerie smiled and squeezed his hand.

"Don't worry about that. We are the Strikeforce Team."

46

Chapter 6

Valerie and her friends – for that is how she thought of Dan now, as they banded together to survive this horrible place - walked down the same cold, stark hallway toward their rooms. They walked slower and slower the further they went, until they dragged their feet along the tiles. Every step required superhuman strength. Did they really have to sleep in those cheerless cells? How long would they have to stay up here in this loony bin?

Not a sound echoed through the building. All the residents were already under lock-down. Dan and the investigators had stayed up late, researching every aspect of the case until they couldn't keep their eyes open any longer. They would have stayed up all night, if they didn't need to get up and continue their investigation in the morning. In the end, Charlene ordered all three of them to bed.

They stopped in front of the first door. Charlene glanced up and down the hall.

"Well, here we are. I guess I'll turn in."

Valerie peered through the door. "There isn't even a sheet on the cot. How do these people stand it?"

Charlene pulled back her shoulders. "The good news is it's only for a little while. Pretty soon we'll go home to our penthouse in Denver and forget this place exists." She clapped her hands and headed for the door. "It's just like camping. How bad can it be?"

She disappeared into the dark room, and Dan and Valerie moved on to the next door. Valerie's shoe still held the door open. The black maw of hopeless despair yawned open and sucked her soul into the bottomless pit. She couldn't really spend the night in there, could she?

She'd been camping before, and it was nothing like this. When she went camping, she had a cheery camp fire to warm her toes and the stars sparkled overhead. She had a nice cozy sleeping bag to climb into when the night got cold, and she had a steaming coffee pot to wake up to in the morning. This was nothing like camping.

Dan stopped in front of the second door and faced her. "I guess this is it."

Valerie sighed. "Yeah."

"I hope to high heaven none of these fruit cakes gets the idea of locking us in our rooms in the middle of the night," he told her. "If they do, I'll be breaking some heads when I wake up in the morning. I just want to warn you ahead of time, seeing as how you're a federal agent and everything."

The tension shattered, and Valerie laughed. "Don't worry. If it comes to that, I'll help you break as many heads as it takes. I'm sure Charlene will help us out, too."

He looked over his shoulder at the black doorway.

"By the way, I want to thank you and your partner for helping me solve my father's murder. I don't know what I would have done if I'd come up here and you weren't here. You're keeping me sane through all this."

She smiled at him, but realised that he might not be able to see her in the dark.

"We're glad to help. We want to break up this racket as much as anybody, and your father did some amazing work before he died. None of this would be possible without him."

Dan nodded.

"I always admired him, but he was ten times the man I thought he was. I never thought he had what it took to go undercover in a place like this. I'll admire him for the rest of my life for that."

"He was a great man," Valerie agreed.

The conversation died, and Valerie shifted from one foot to the other. She rubbed her arms for warmth, but she sure wasn't going to find it in that room. She would stay out in this hall as long as she could.

"I meant to tell you," Dan went on, "I'm really impressed with the way you're running this investigation. The way you question people is a sight to see. You get the information out of them without intimidating them, and somehow you go straight to the heart of the matter with no trouble. You're making great strides. You'll have this case solved in no time."

Valerie snorted. "Not fast enough to save me from spending a night in that hole."

Dan laughed, and the sound warmed her heart. He drove all the hopeless demons out of her mind. She could almost enjoy this place with him in it. "That's a good one."

Valerie fidgeted. "I guess we'd better get to sleep."

"Yeah." His breathing filled the silence.

"Good night." She took a step toward the room.

Dan stepped in front of her. She hadn't expected him to move so fast. "Wait."

"What's the matter?" she asked.

He fidgeted. "Don't go just yet."

Valerie gave a shaky laugh. "Okay."

He looked up and down the hall. "I don't want to go to sleep just yet. Let's stay up a little longer."

"Okay," she replied. "What do you want to do?"

A tense silence followed. Then he spoke. "I don't know. I just don't want to.... you know. I just don't want to say good night just yet."

"Okay." She was starting to sound like a broken record. "I don't want to say good night, either."

His head whipped around. "You don't?"

"No, I don't," she replied. "I like talking to you."

"You do?" His voice soared.

"Sure, I do," she replied. "You're a nice guy, aren't you? And who else do I have to talk to around here besides Charlene."

His shoulders sagged. "Oh. Okay."

"Do you... I mean, what should we.... do you....?" She trailed off.

All of a sudden, she realized he was staring at her through the darkness. His breath whispered in and out through his nose. "I never met anyone like you before, Valerie. You're some piece of work."

Valerie snickered. "I guess you never met any federal agents before."

He shook his head. "It's not that. I never met a woman as strong and smart and easy-going as you. I wish we could spend some time together when we're not working on a murder case."

Valerie tried, again, to dispel her nervousness by joking. "It's too bad you live in Phoenix and I live in Denver."

He shook his head again. "I would travel to the ends of the earth to spend time with a woman like you."

She shifted on her feet again. "You're just saying that."

He took a step toward her. "There's only one thing to do. We'll have to spend time together up here."

"We're already spending twenty-four hours a day together," she pointed out. "We're almost joined at the hip."

"Not exactly," he replied. "But we could be."

She caught her breath, but before she could answer, he leaned over and kissed her. His lips locked onto hers, and his warm breath filled her nostrils.

A rush of warmth spread over her face and down into her body. His face blocked out the tiny shred of light coming from the main entrance of the building, so she didn't need to keep her eyes open anymore.

As her eyes slid closed, passion and fatigue washed over her. She melted against him, and he enfolded her in his arms. At least Charlene wasn't there to see her. Her mouth opened, and his tongue slipped into her mouth. In an instant, their tongues were dancing and rolling together between their lips, and Dan's hands slid deliciously over every part of her body.

Valerie wrapped her arms around his neck and clung to him suddenly unable to stand. He scooped her up and carried her into the last open room, the one farthest away from Charlene. He set her down in the corner near the cot, and in the dark, their bodies took over where their minds left off.

Dan pressed Valerie against his body, and the power of his passion rippled from one to the other. His hands ran down her sides to her hips, and a quiver shot through her. She couldn't hold herself back from responding to him, and she wouldn't even try. Her legs shook and the movement rubbed her against his body.

He stroked the sides of her thighs, and her breath came short and uneven as his clever hands removed her clothing in the dark. How long did she have to stand here and hold herself together before she exploded into a torrent of excitement? All of a sudden, he picked her up. In one swoop, he hoisted her into his arms. Her legs wrapped themselves around his waist, and they disappeared into each other in the delicious dark.

Chapter 7

Valerie sat in Sri Danke's office chair and tapped at her computer while Charlene worked on her laptop. Dan sat across the room and brooded. Valerie scrolled through acres of federal documents. "It's all here. Every dirty trick EdenCloud ever pulled, and Harold Henderson was the witness behind it all. He filed dozens of affidavits about their shenanigans, but his cover was never blown. I wonder how long Colonel Tomlinson intended to keep him here before he busted EdenCloud wide open."

"Can you ask him?" Dan asked.

"I already did," Valerie replied. "I sent him an email asking for your father's file. I haven't heard back from him yet."

"There's one thing I don't understand," Charlene put in. "The investigation implicates Barbara McGregor, but not Charles Farnsworth. In fact, none of the other administrators are listed as suspects."

"Maybe they're working undercover, too," Dan suggested.

Valerie closed her computer.

"I'm going to interview them. They'll be finished with breakfast now, so we better catch them before they go back to their rooms."

Dan peered out the office door. "They aren't going back to their rooms. They're going outside."

Valerie came to his side. "They must be going out to work or for some other activity."

"Look." Charlene pointed to the dining room. "There goes Butterfly Wing. Let's grab him first."

Butterfly Wing stood next to Sri Danke near the dining room entrance, but they separated when the investigators approached. "I hope you found what you were looking for."

"We did," Valerie replied. "We found out quite a bit of very useful information about Woodpecker and Firehawk and Donner and Blitzen and all the rest of the reindeer, too."

He narrowed his eyes at her.

"I hope you're not making a joke out of our names. We're here to evolve spiritually, not to provide you with cheap humor."

"I would never make a joke out of what goes on here," Valerie replied. "That's what we want to talk to you about."

"Then go ahead and talk," he told her. "I have things to do."

"How well did you know Firehawk?" she asked.

"How well did any of us know Firehawk?" he returned.

"None of us can really know anyone else. We can only know their superficial coil, the mortal part of them confined to this earth while life lasts. No one can really know the eternal soul inside."

Valerie shrugged. "I'm talking about the mortal part of Firehawk confined to this earth. What did you know about him?"

"Not very much," Butterfly Wing replied. "We don't socialize much up here. We concentrate on our spiritual development and shun the ordinary aspects of life."

"Sri Danke said Firehawk was a spiritual leader and the other residents would bow to him and ask his advice," Valerie told him. "Do you know what sort of advice he gave them?"

Butterfly Wing shook his head. "I never consulted him myself."

"Did you ask any of the others what they consulted him about?" Valerie asked.

He shook his head again.

"That sort of conversation isn't encouraged around here. We stick to ourselves. No one can know what development one person needs to reach their spiritual potential. But if you want to know what advice Firehawk gave people, you should ask Featherbright."

"Featherbright!" Valerie repeated. "That's one of the administrators, isn't it?"

"That's right," Butterfly Wing replied. "He spent hours with Firehawk outside under his tree. If anybody knows what Firehawk told his followers, Featherbright will."

Valerie regarded him with her head on one side. "That's an interesting way of putting it."

"What do you mean?" he asked.

"You called the people who consulted Firehawk his followers," she told him. "I imagine Firehawk having followers posed a threat to EdenCloud. Certain people could get very angry over that."

Butterfly Wing shrugged. "I don't think so. Firehawk couldn't do anything to threaten EdenCloud, and no one here would get angry over anything he did. We're better than that."

Valerie turned away. "Okay. So they didn't get angry, but EdenCloud is a multimillion dollar operation. Anything that interfered with that operation would not be taken lightly. I'm certain of that."

Butterfly Wing nodded toward the main entrance. "There goes Featherbright now."

Valerie glanced over her shoulder just in time to see a young man in glasses slip through the door and disappear outside. "Just one more question. Can you tell me where you were when Firehawk was killed?"

"I was in the kitchen," he replied. "I'm in charge of the kitchen crew, so I'm in there every day to supervise the cooking and the clean-up. Half a dozen other souls were there with me. They can confirm I didn't kill him."

Valerie nodded. "Thank you. I'm glad to finally meet one innocent person."

Butterfly Wing turned back into the dining room, and Valerie and her friends strolled out of the building. The crisp mountain sunshine dazzled their eyes, and they paused on the steps to let their eyes adjust.

Valerie nodded to a row of orange-clad figures in front of the trees. "There's Featherbright."

The young man that Butterfly Wing had pointed out looked over his shoulder at the investigators at that moment. Then he turned around and buried his head in whatever the residents were doing over there. "How should we tackle him?" Valerie asked. "All three of us marching right up to him might intimidate him. Maybe only one of us should go."

"You go, Valerie," Charlene told her. "You've taken the lead on this case, and you've done a bang-up job so far. Besides, you're the smallest of the three of us. People don't get as intimidated by you as they do by me."

Valerie snorted. "Maybe that's why you should be interviewing the suspects."

Charlene smiled. "I'll go back to the office with Dan. Meet us there when you're done and tell us what you've found out about Featherbright's meetings with Firehawk."

Valerie waited until her friends went back inside before she sauntered up to the residents. She poked her head between their shoulders. "What are you doing?"

A scuffling silence answered her. In the end, Featherbright spoke up. "We're breaking the ground for a new garden bed. We grow all our own food, and we need another garlic bed."

"Do you grow all the lentils for the dahl and the chickpeas for the hummus, too?" Valerie asked.

Featherbright shifted from one foot to the other. "No, we order them from a distributor in Chicago."

"But it's all organic, right?" Valerie asked. "You wouldn't eat anything that's not organic."

Featherbright cast a quick glance at his companions. "No, the lentils and chickpeas aren't organic, and neither is the spinach. We buy that in frozen and thaw it out."

Valerie gasped. "Really? I'm surprised. I thought EdenCloud was all about spiritual purity and that stuff. I didn't think you would have anything to do with something not organic."

"I should know if it's organic or not," Featherbright replied. "I do all the ordering for the kitchen."

Valerie examined him. "You're Featherbright, aren't you? Butterfly Wing told me about you. I'd like to ask you some questions about Firehawk if you don't mind."

He glanced at his fellow inmates again. They stole furtive peeks at him over Valerie's shoulder. "I don't know anything about Firehawk."

"But you're one of the administrators," Valerie pointed out. "You must know more than the others about his background, how long he was coming to EdenCloud, all that sort of thing. I would really appreciate if you would....."

"I told you I don't know anything about Firehawk," he snapped. "Is there something wrong with your ears?"

Valerie stared at him. Featherbright blushed at his own outburst and bent over the rough sod at his feet. He broke it up with a pitchfork. Valerie looked over her shoulder at the other residents, but they all kept their heads down. "Come with me, Featherbright. Let's take a walk down to the stream over there and talk."

"No," he grumbled.

Valerie took a deep breath. "If you don't come, I'll place you under arrest and drive you to Santa Fe. You can answer my questions at the police station if you prefer."

Featherbright let out an exasperated sigh and threw his pitchfork on the ground. He stomped off to the stream and left Valerie behind. She hurried after him and found him sitting on a big flat rock in the shade overlooking a still pool. He tore blades of grass out of the ground, ripped them into pieces, and tossed the pieces into the water.

Valerie watched him for a while before she spoke. "That's not really a very spiritually evolved thing to do. You're killing the poor defenseless grass plants."

"I don't give a crap if I kill them," he shot back. "I'm hungry and I want to go home. I want a roast beef sandwich with a big scoop of strawberry ice cream, but I'll probably never get it again as long as I live."

Valerie's eyes widened. "Can't you just leave?"

"How am I supposed to leave?" he asked.

Valerie waved her hand at the expensive cars in the parking lot. "Don't you have a car?"

"I don't have a car," he replied. "Firehawk gave me a ride up here from Albuquerque, and now he's dead. I'm stuck here. I can't even send an email or make a phone call to my parents to let them know I'm all right. If I could, I would ask them to come and get me, or at least send me a bus ticket. I would walk to Santa Fe if it meant getting out of this place."

"Listen, Featherbright...." Valerie began.

He rounded on her with his teeth clenched. "Stop calling me that stupid name! My name is Jacob, not Featherbright. I'm Jacob Duncan. Do you hear me? Jacob Duncan!"

Valerie stared at him in amazement. "All right, Jacob. I'm sorry. It's impossible to tell who is sane in this place, but if you really want to get out of here, we'll take you with us when we leave. We'll make sure you get home safely."

His head shot up. "Do you really mean that?"

"Of course," she replied. "We're federal agents. We wouldn't leave you here against your will. We'll have Firehawk's murder solved pretty soon, and then we'll take you home to your roast beef sandwich."

His eyes lit up. "Thanks."

"Now," she went on, "I'm glad I finally found someone willing to talk sense because I need to ask you some hard questions about Firehawk."

"You can call him by his real name," Jacob replied. "I know all about Mr. Henderson and how he was undercover up here to bust EdenCloud. He told me all about it."

Valerie gulped. "He did?"

Jacob nodded. "What do you think he was doing, sitting under a tree for days on end? He was trying to get people to realize how corrupt and evil the administrators are. He was trying to get them to fight back and break free. He was the only person in this whole crazy place who really cared about freedom."

"But you are one of the administrators," Valerie pointed out.

He shook his head. "Sri Danke made me take on the job of ordering the food and linen and everything else. I didn't want to, but then Mr. Henderson told me I could do some good by finding out as much as I could about how the place runs. He asked me to testify against the organization when it came to things like ordering non-organic food."

"What do you mean?" Valerie asked. "What would you testify about?"

"It says right there on everybody's invoice," he told her. "When you sign up for one of EdenCloud's residential development programs, it says right there on the invoice that organic meals are included. They charge extra for organic food, and then they order non-organic food. It's fraud and everybody knows it, but no one will do anything about it. Mr. Henderson said I did the ordering so my testimony would help the case against EdenCloud."

"What else did Mr. Henderson tell you?" she asked.

"It wasn't just me," Jacob replied. "He said the same thing to everyone who would listen to him. He said we came up here to get free, and these people kept us prisoner. He said the only way we could get truly free was to throw them over and put them in prison instead."

He burst into hysterical laughter. His shoulders shook, but then he dropped his head, and tears fell into the dust under his feet. "And now he's dead. They killed him."

"Do you have any idea who killed him?" Valerie asked.

"It could only be Sri Danke," he replied. "She's as crooked as they come, and she runs the whole operation. She hated him for trying to help people."

"She said she didn't know what he was telling people out there under his tree," Valerie told him. "Did she find out somehow?"

"I don't see how she could have missed it," he replied.

"She's got spies all over the place, and Mr. Henderson never minced his words. He didn't care who was around. He would talk the same rebellion even when he knew for certain someone would rat him out to Sri Danke. He shot Sri Danke the big middle finger. She could do her worst and let her come and try. That was his attitude."

Valerie sighed. "It sounds like she did."

Jacob closed his eyes, and tears trickled down his cheeks.

"You're a nice person. I can tell. Mr. Henderson said the same thing about taking me home, but he never got a chance."

Valerie laid her hand on his shoulder. "Don't worry, Jacob. You won't have to stay here anymore. Can you tell me anything else about the night Mr. Henderson was killed? Did you see anything in the dining room?"

He shook his head. "I came out of my room when the bell sounded, the same way I always do, but there were already dozens of people there before me. I couldn't understand it. They were all standing around the doorway, and I went over to see what was going on. That's when I saw his body lying on the ground."

Valerie frowned. "Was he already dead when the bell went off?"

"He was stone cold and very white," he replied, "all except for the marks around his neck."

"Did you ask the others about it?" she asked. "Did the people standing around see what happened?"

"We all started talking at once," he replied, "even though we're not supposed to. None of them saw anything. They all did the same thing I did. They came out of their rooms and found him dead."

Valerie jumped up. "Thank you very much for your help, Jacob. I'm going back inside now to find my partner, but don't forget what I said. As soon as this case is over, we're getting you out of here. Remember that."

He only had time to break into a grateful smile before Valerie hurried away. Her mind churned with a dozen possibilities, and she ran up the steps two at a time to the entrance.

64

Chapter 8

Valerie burst into Sri Danke's office and startled Dan out of a doze. He hadn't slept much last night. Then again, neither had Valerie. Charlene would be furious if she found out that they'd stayed up all night together. "I've got it!"

Dan rubbed his eyes. "You've got what?"

"The smoking gun," Valerie crowed.

Charlene looked up from her computer. "So do you know who killed Firehawk?"

Valerie wilted. "Not exactly. But I've figured out who was in on it."

"Let me guess," Dan growled. "It was the head honcho herself, Barbara whatshername."

Valerie grinned. "If she didn't strangle him herself, she definitely had something to do with it. Take a look at that."

She pointed to a panel on the wall.

A row of numbered lights glowed on the panel. Under each light, another darkened row of indicators matched the first.

"What are we looking at?" Charlene asked.

"These numbers correspond to the residents' rooms," Valerie told her. "The lights that are turned on indicate the power supply to each room, and the lights underneath indicate whether the door is open or closed. They're all turned off right now because the residents are out of their rooms."

"So what does that tell us?" Dan asked.

"This is Sri Danke's office," Valerie explained. "She controls when the residents' doors open and when they lock. She controls their every move. She controls their very lives."

"That doesn't mean she killed Harold Henderson," Charlene countered.

"I just talked to Featherbright," Valerie told her. "His real name is Jacob Duncan, and he wants out. Henderson recruited him to testify against EdenCloud because he orders the food for the center and knows about instances of fraud and false accounting. He says Henderson was dead and cold before anybody came out of their rooms for dinner."

Charlene frowned. "But that's impossible. If all their doors were locked, how could anybody come out to kill him?"

Valerie pointed at her. "My point exactly. One of two things happened. Either Sri Danke strangled him herself...."

"I find that hard to believe," Charlene interrupted. "Miss High-and-Mighty wouldn't soil her hands with that."

"I agree with you," Valerie replied. "That leaves only one option. Sri Danke ordered someone else to kill Henderson, and she arranged to open the killer's door, so that person could come out and strangle him in the dining room, when no one else was around."

"That doesn't bring us any closer to finding out who that person was," Charlene pointed out. "She could open any door she wanted. That leaves us with a couple of hundred possibilities."

Valerie sank into a chair. "I know."

Charlene sighed. "What else did this Jacob Duncan tell you?"

Valerie straightened up. "I don't want to talk about Jacob anymore right now. The best thing we can do for Jacob and all the other poor fools stuck in this place is to solve the case as fast as we can. We still have one more person to interview."

"Who?" Charlene asked.

"AngelPie," Valerie replied.

Charlene snickered, and Dan cleared his throat.

"Whoever this AngelPie is, she's the last of the administrators," Valerie went on. "She can probably give us the one piece of the puzzle we need to crack this case once and for all."

"How do you know AngelPie is female?" Dan asked.

Valerie rounded on him. "You don't think any male would pick a name like AngelPie, do you?"

His mouth twisted into a wry grin. "You wouldn't think any male would pick a name like Butterfly Wing, would you? Or Snowdrop?"

Valerie grinned back. "Okay. You got me there. Either way, we have to find AngelPie."

"What about Snowdrop?" Charlene asked. "Don't you want to find him, too?"

"Once we figure out who killed Henderson," Valerie replied, "we can shut the whole place down. Once we do that, we'll be able to find Snowdrop with no problem."

Charlene shut her computer and stood up. "All right. Let's go."

At that moment, Sri Danke came into the office.

"Oh, there you are, Ms. McGregor," Charlene exclaimed. "We were just coming to find you. We'd like you to introduce us to AngelPie. She's the last administrator we have to interview. Hopefully, once we get that done, we can get out of your hair."

Sri Danke frowned. Charlene chuckled. "Sorry. Bad joke."

Sri Danke pursed her lips. "I don't appreciate your jokes, and I don't appreciate you using that name. I told you before we...."

Charlene held up her hand. "I know what you told me before, but I'm not playing games anymore. I checked your federal income tax returns for the last ten years, and you have never stopped using the name Barbara McGregor. If it's good enough for the IRS, it's good enough for me. We aren't dealing with your immortal soul in the spirit world. We're dealing with a flesh and blood man who had the life strangled out of him by a flesh and blood killer. If you didn't kill him, you know who did. So will you kindly show us where we can find AngelPie? I have a feeling someone is leaving here in handcuffs before the day is over."

Sri Danke glared at her, and for the first time, her serene composure failed her. Valerie shivered. This woman was a stone cold killer. Valerie was never so sure of anything in her life. She and her friends had to solve this case and get out of there before someone else wound up dead.

Sri Danke turned away. "Follow me."

Dan and Valerie jumped out of their chairs, and all three hurried after Sri Danke. She didn't lead them back to the gardening project out front, the way Valerie expected her to. From the front steps, one robed figure looked exactly like another, but Jacob Duncan must be back down there somewhere.

Instead, Sri Danke turned a corner towards the back of the building, but she didn't stop there. She strode up the hill behind the center, and into the trees. The path twisted and turned one way and then the other. Charlene fell in behind Sri Danke. Valerie came behind her, and Dan brought up the rear. In a moment, the whole group was breathing heavily with the steep climb.

Sri Danke stopped at the top of the hill. The breeze blew into their faces, and the wide rolling mountains of the Northern New Mexico wilderness stretched out before them, as far as the eye could see. Sri Danke caught her breath and pointed. "There. That's AngelPie."

Far below them, a bright orange speck flitted through a field of wild flowers. The sun shone off a bald head, and the faint wisp of a human voice rose on the wind to reach Valerie's ears.

The speck inched through the grass and flowers, but at that distance the group couldn't make out any other details of this mysterious person. Before any of them could think to ask, Sri Danke turned on her heel and strode back down the path the way they had come. The three of them were left standing alone on the mountain top, with nothing but the vast expanse of empty country on all sides.

Charlene sighed. "Well, let's go see this AngelPie."

She started down the other side of the hill, and Dan and Valerie followed. No path cut through that rough landscape, so they had to bushwack their way down the slope. In some places, they had to sidestep down steep banks and switch back over gravel fields. The voice in the wild flowers grew louder, and after a while, Valerie realized that the strange person was singing. At last, they dropped down into the field where AngelPie moved from one patch of color to the next.

Charlene panted for breath and wiped the sweat from her upper lip. She strode up to AngelPie and stopped. The investigators examined their subject for the first time. AngelPie was, in fact, a woman — or, more accurately, a young girl. Her bald head couldn't hide the fresh, innocent face underneath, and she smiled at them.

"You must be AngelPie," Charlene began.

AngelPie smiled, but she didn't answer. She went on singing in her rather squeaky voice.

Charlene cleared her throat. "Sri Danke said we could talk to you about Firehawk. Do you mind if we ask you some questions about him?"

AngelPie turned up her face into the sunshine. "Isn't it beautiful here? I just love this place. I come here every day, rain or shine. It gives me an idea of what heaven must be like."

"Did you ever talk to Firehawk when he used to sit out under his tree?" Charlene asked. "Did you ever hear what he said to other people about what they should do here at EdenCloud?"

"I never talked to Firehawk," AngelPie replied. "Sri Danke tells me what to do. I listen to her, and she frees me from the shackles of the world."

Charlene waved her hand at the flowers. "But this place is part of the world. You don't want to be freed from this, do you?"

"There's a light.... in the darkness..... of every... body's life," she sang.

Valerie frowned. Where had she heard those words before?

"So you never talked to Firehawk," Charlene went on.

"Could you tell us what duties you perform as one of the administrators of EdenCloud?"

"EdenCloud is the most wonderful place on Earth," AngelPie told them. "Everybody who comes here breaks free from the corruption of the material world and experiences the bliss and tranquility of heaven. I should know. I've been coming here for fifteen years."

Charlene's head whipped around. "Fifteen years! But you can't be much older than that now."

AngelPie closed her eyes and sang in falsetto. "Far away.... across the sea.... my love is waiting for me...."

Valerie broke in on the conversation. "How old are you, AngelPie?"

"I'm seventeen." She broke into a radiant smile. "I'm the youngest soul at EdenCloud. Isn't that wonderful? EdenCloud is all I've ever known. I'm the most enlightened soul here. Just a little bit more spiritual development, and I'll break free of my mortal shell and rise into the heavens." She closed her eyes and took a deep breath of the pure mountain air. "I can't wait for that to happen."

"If you're seventeen," Valerie remarked, "and you've been coming here for fifteen years, you must have come here for the first time when you were two years old."

"That's right," she replied. "My mother brought me here, and I've lived here ever since. This is my home, and when I leave here, I'll rise to my celestial home in the stars." She raised her hands to the sky. "I'll drift on the clouds and sing with the angels. I'm almost there now. My mother says so."

Puzzle pieces clicked into place in Valerie's mind. "Is your mother Sri Danke?"

AngelPie smiled. "Yes. Isn't that wonderful? Aren't I the luckiest soul in the world, to have such an evolved and blessed soul for a mother? Imagine how evolved I must be, how advanced my soul must be, to be born to a mother who would bring me here and raise me here. I can't imagine how awful my life would have been if I'd been born to ordinary parents and never had the chance to experience the bliss of EdenCloud."

Dan turned away with a grimace. "I can only imagine."

Charlene took a deep breath and tried again. "We really need to ask you about Firehawk. Can you think about Firehawk for a minute, AngelPie? We're here to investigate his death, and we have to ask you some questions. Is that all right?"

"I'll keep rolling along..." she sang. "Tumbling on with the tumbling tumbleweeds."

Dan turned to Valerie and grumbled under his breath.

"This is hopeless. Let's get out of here."

"Can you tell us where you were when Firehawk was killed?" Charlene asked. "Can you remember where you were and what you were doing at the time?"

For the first time, a shadow crossed AngelPie's face. "Firehawk.... is dead?"

Charlene sucked in her breath. "Didn't you know? He was strangled outside the dining room. You must have known. Everybody at EdenCloud knows."

The shadow passed, and the radiant smile returned to AngelPie's face. "When you see..... the moon hanging over the prairie...." She closed her eyes in the pure joy of singing.

Charlene turned away.

"I give up. Let's go back to the center."

Charlene and Dan started up the hill the way they'd come, but Valerie hung back. She couldn't take her eyes off the young girl. If she'd had hair on her head and regular clothes on, she would have looked just like every other girl in the world.

She would have looked peaceful and contented, picking flowers in the meadow.

Chapter 9

Charlene stopped on the steps in front of the entrance.

"Well, that was a complete waste of time. AngelPie won't tell us anything. She won't betray her mother."

"Maybe she can't tell us anything," Dan suggested. "She's out of her mind. I'm not surprised. She's been locked up here all her life with that witch for a mother. She belongs in a padded room."

"She might not be out of her mind," Valerie told him.

"Did you see how dark her gums were? They were dark purple, almost black. That's a sign of severe B vitamin deficiency. She's been eating this horrible food all her life, without any meat, dairy, eggs, fish, or any other source of B vitamins. That could explain why her mind isn't working right."

"That doesn't bring us any closer to solving Harold Henderson's murder," Charlene pointed out.

"Whether she can't, or she won't, tell us anything, we're right back to square one. Anybody have any suggestions?"

"She did tell us one thing we didn't know before," Valerie replied.

"She told us Sri Danke was her mother. Let's go back to the office. We might find some record of them. If Sri Danke brought a two-year-old up here, some of the other residents might have done the same thing. They might have been investigated for neglect or abuse."

Charlene shuddered. "Don't even suggest that."

"It's worth looking into," Valerie told her. "Raising a growing child on a diet of dahl, hummus, and frozen spinach doesn't exactly meet the standard of providing for their needs."

The others didn't answer, but followed her in silence back to Sri Danke's office. At that moment, however, the deafening siren sounded and dozens of orange-clad inmates flooded into the center. They wound their way up the halls and disappeared into their rooms.

Valerie glanced into Sri Danke's office and found the woman standing over her control panel. "Locking your prisoners in for the day?"

Sri Danke looked up. "I don't know what you're talking about."

Valerie pointed to the panel. "That's what I'm talking about. You, and only you, control who goes in and who goes out. You, and only you, control who is free to walk around and who must stay in their rooms for meditation and reflection. It must give you a sick thrill to control people's lives like that. At least we know that you, and only you, decided who to let out of their room in time to kill Firehawk before dinner. You were the mastermind behind his murder. Admit it."

Sri Danke stared at her. Then she pointed to the panel, too. "Do you see that? That's an electronic timer. The doors lock and unlock automatically. The security company that installed the mechanism programmed the computer to open and close the doors. I can't override the program. I have no more idea who killed Firehawk than you do."

Valerie's shoulders slumped. "Oh. I didn't know that."

Sri Danke sighed. "It was an honest mistake. I'm in charge of this center, so naturally you thought I could have let someone out of their room to kill Firehawk. But I didn't. Someone must have jammed their door open the same way you did to stop it from locking. Then, when no one was around, they came out and killed Firehawk. It's the only explanation."

Valerie brightened up. "Hey, that reminds me. If everyone was locked into their rooms at the time, what was Firehawk doing out? What was he doing in the dining room at that time? Shouldn't he have been locked down, too?"

"I told you before," Sri Danke replied. "He just came in from his tree. He used to sit out there for days at a time, expounding on.... whatever it was he was expounding on. None of us knew when he would decide to come inside, but he decided right then. He just walked in, and the next thing we knew he was dead."

Charlene shook her head. "It couldn't have happened like that. There must have been someone else who knew what he was doing and where he was going."

Another siren went off, and the din of hundreds of doors locking echoed through the building.

At the same moment, a line of figures came through the front entrance and filed into the dining room. Butterfly Wing met them at the door and counted off their heads as they passed him.

"Who are they?" Charlene asked. "What are they doing out of their rooms?"

"That's the kitchen crew," Sri Danke replied. "They're on their way to make lunch. At the next bell, the other souls will come out of their rooms to eat, so they have to make the food now."

Valerie whipped around. "But that means the kitchen workers were out of their rooms when Firehawk was killed. One of them could have left the kitchen and killed him."

"That wouldn't work," Charlene countered. "Butterfly Wing told us he was in the kitchen at the time. He said everyone was accounted for, and he would have noticed if anyone had disappeared in the middle of the shift."

"I'm going to check anyway." Valerie started toward the dining room.

Dan and Charlene hurried after her, and they found Butterfly Wing in the kitchen. He gave his crew their orders. When he finished, they broke up and went to their tasks, leaving him with the investigators. "Can I help you with something?"

"We just want to ask you some more questions about the day Firehawk was killed," Valerie told him.

"I already told you I was here," Butterfly Wing replied. "The whole crew can confirm that."

"We know you're innocent," Valerie replied. "It's the rest of your crew we want to know about. One of them must have snuck out of the kitchen to kill Firehawk. They were the only people out of their rooms at the time."

Butterfly Wing shook his head. "That's impossible. I run a tight ship around here. None of them could have left without me noticing. I know every soul in this place, and I keep track of my crew while they're working in the kitchen. I can confirm they were all here."

"Well, someone must have killed him," Valerie pointed out. "Your crew was perfectly positioned to see him come back into the center from outside. Everybody else was locked in their rooms."

Butterfly Wing pursed his lips. "You don't believe me? Here's the roster. You can look for yourselves." He grabbed a tattered clipboard from a nail on the wall and shoved it at her. Valerie stared at it in surprise. Then he started thumbing through the pages. "I'll show you. Here it is. This is the dinner roster for the day Firehawk was killed. You can see for yourself who checked in and when they checked out. No one had time to sneak out and kill Firehawk." He shoved the clipboard into her hands.

Valerie stared down at the smudged page. Her eye skimmed down the list of names. "But AngelPie is on this list, and there's no mark next to her name."

Butterfly Wing stared at her. Then he swallowed. "Well, no. She doesn't come for shifts, not even when she's rostered. She comes and goes as she pleases. She's.... she's different, you know."

"Yeah, I know," Valerie replied. "So she was out of her room at the time Firehawk was killed? She was let out to work on the kitchen crew, but she didn't come."

"You don't understand," Butterfly Wing replied. "She's always out of her room. She's never locked down. She comes and goes as she pleases."

Valerie exchanged glances with her friends. Then she shoved the clipboard back into his hands. "Thank you. You've been very helpful."

Chapter 10

The investigators strode out of the dining room. "Now what are we going to do?" Charlene asked. "How are we going to find that girl again? She could be anywhere in these mountains."

"The question is," Valerie returned, "how are we going to arrest her for murder? She probably has no memory of doing it."

The sound of voices brought their attention back to the office. The voices rose and fell in anger, and one young female voice shouted above the other. It sounded exactly like any ordinary teenager yelling at her mother.

"You don't care about me. You never did. I gave up everything for you, and this is how you treat me. I hate you. I'll hate you until the end of the world."

The investigators snuck up to the office and peeked around the door. AngelPie leaned over her mother's desk, and no one would have recognized her face. Black rage had taken the place of her serene, airy contentment. Not even the stray wisp of grass in her hair could make her look as angelic as she had in the meadow.

"You can hate me all you like, AngelPie," Sri Danke replied.

"It doesn't change the fact that you did something wrong. Now you have to pay for it."

"I'm not going to pay for it," AngelPie shot back.

"I did it for you, and now you want to throw me to the dogs — and for what? For some man! That snark was right about you. I should have listened to him when he said you would use this to make the rest of us suffer. But I was stupid. I tried to protect you, and now you're shoving it in my face. You must be happy to have such a stupid daughter."

Valerie stepped into the room.

"What's going on? Is this anything we should know about?"

Sri Danke waved her hand.

"It's nothing. AngelPie's a little upset about something. That's all. She'll settle down in a minute, and then we can all go back to working on our spiritual development."

"Don't listen to her, lady," AngelPie cried.

"She's never worked on her spiritual development in her life. She sits in here, working on her accounts, while the rest of the souls pray and meditate and work to put money into her pocket. She's rotten to the core. Firehawk was right about that, but I was too stupid to listen."

"You said you never had anything to do with Firehawk," Valerie pointed out. "Did you talk to him after all?"

"I never talked to him," AngelPie replied.

She had a wild look about her as she went on.

"I didn't have to. All I had to do was hear what he said to everybody else. No one around here pays any attention to me. They act like I don't exist, and Firehawk was no different. He talked up a storm right in front of me. He didn't care if I heard or not."

"What did he say about your mother?" Charlene asked. "What did he say about her being rotten?"

"He said all kinds of things," AngelPie replied. "But only one thing mattered to me. He came in from outside one time. He'd been out there for three weeks straight, so no one expected him to come in. He came in right before the work period, so everyone was in their rooms. He heard a strange sound coming from this office, so he came to see what it was."

Valerie glanced at Sri Danke. "What did he see?"

AngelPie pointed an accusing finger at her mother. "He saw her, spreading her body open to that man!"

Valerie gasped. "Man! What man?"

"Butterfly Wing!" AngelPie shrieked. "She rutted around with Butterfly Wing while the other souls were locked in their rooms. She never even tried to evolve or perfect herself. It was all an act to make a pile of money."

"And Firehawk found out about it," Valerie concluded. "No wonder they killed him."

"They didn't kill him," AngelPie shrieked. "I did! I killed him with my bare hands for saying those nasty things about her. I did it to protect her."

"But he was telling the truth, AngelPie," Charlene murmured. "He said nasty things, but they were true things. She really is rotten and corrupt. She really is using these people to line her own pocket."

"Don't you think I know that?" AngelPie cried. "Who do you think knows that better than I do? Firehawk was going to destroy her, and everything she's built up here. He was going to ruin EdenCloud."

"And EdenCloud is the only home you've ever had," Valerie replied. "I understand now."

AngelPie looked from one face to the next. Her voice rose to a screech. "What was going to happen to me when EdenCloud went under? Where was I going to go? Who would take care of me? I might wind up in police custody, or worse yet, foster care! What if they tried to make me eat meat? I would lose my chance to rise to heaven. I would be stuck here on this filthy little planet for the rest of my life."

Valerie took a step toward her. She put out her hand to touch her arm, but AngelPie drew back in horror. "Don't touch me!"

Valerie held up her hands.

"All right, AngelPie. It's going to be all right. We'll make sure you're taken care of and no one tries to make you eat any meat."

AngelPie panted for breath. Little squeaks of emotion came out of her mouth, but she couldn't manage to talk anymore. She kept glancing around the room from one person to another. Sri Danke hung her head.

Charlene stepped forward. "Did you know about this? Did you know that she killed Firehawk?"

Sri Danke shook her head. "I suspected it might be her. She was the only one out of her room at the time, and the kitchen crew were all accounted for. Then she started yelling at me about Butterfly Wing. She could only have found out about it from Firehawk, so I thought she might have.... you know."

Valerie took AngelPie by the arm, and this time, the girl didn't fight back. "Come with us, AngelPie. We'll make sure you're taken care of."

AngelPie blinked. She looked smaller all of a sudden. "You won't put me in foster care, will you?"

"I don't think you'll be put in foster care," Valerie replied. "I think you'll go to a special place where you can rest and heal from this. There are lots of people in the world who want to help you, and lots of nice places you can go. You're going to be all right. I promise."

Charlene led Sri Danke out of the office and sat her on a bench in the main foyer. She took out her phone. "Dang. No reception."

"Call from the office," Valerie suggested.

Charlene called Colonel Tomlinson, who scrambled three choppers to EdenCloud. Valerie sat AngelPie in a chair across from the desk. "I'll drive you down to Santa Fe myself. I know a woman there who helps people like you."

AngelPie raised her eyes to Valerie's face. She was already slipping back into the haze of dreamy disconnection from the world. "People like me?"

"Yes, AngelPie," Valerie replied. "There are other people like you, and you have a lot in common with them. The woman I'm thinking of runs an organization called HomeFree. It helps people like you make the transition from EdenCloud to.... to a more meaningful life."

AngelPie smiled. "Okay. That sounds all right. Maybe I won't lose my chance to get to heaven after all."

Valerie smiled back at her. "No, you won't."

She turned her attention to the panel. "There must be a way to activate these locks. It can't all be hands off."

She touched the panel, and at that moment, the siren went off. Dan jumped three feet into the air. "What did you do?"

"I didn't do anything," Valerie replied. "Here they come."

Charlene pushed Valerie to the door. "Go talk to them. Tell them the party's over."

Valerie strode out to the foyer and held up her hands to the crowd of inmates. They stole glances at Sri Danke sitting nearby, but no one said anything. Valerie climbed up onto a bench and raised her voice.

"You all know Firehawk wanted to shut EdenCloud down," she began, "and some of you know why. Sri Danke and the EdenCloud organization has been investigated and found guilty of dozens of crimes, including kidnapping, fraud, money laundering, and many others. What you probably didn't know is that Firehawk was an undercover agent, and he found enough evidence to indict Sri Danke and many others."

The inmates exchanged worried glances.

"AngelPie, or whatever her real name is, killed Firehawk to protect her mother," Valerie went on. "We're taking both of them into custody, and we'll be taking a few of you with us to testify against EdenCloud. The rest of you are free to go. EdenCloud no longer exists. Go back to your homes and your families and start the work of rebuilding your lives. If you like, I can put you in touch with an organization called HomeFree that helps people like you get out of groups like EdenCloud."

The crowd started to break up, and one or two people headed for the front entrance.

"There's just one more thing I need you to help me do before you leave," Valerie called out.

They stopped and turned toward her.

"I need you to help me find a man named Snowdrop," Valerie told them. "We don't know where he is, but he has information we need to stop EdenCloud from harming anyone else. Help us find him, and then you're free to go."

Jacob Duncan spoke up from the back of the crowd. "I know where Snowdrop is."

"You do?" Valerie asked.

"Sure," he replied. "He's right here."

Valerie stared at him. This couldn't be happening. The case couldn't end as easily as that.

"Follow me," he told her. "I'll take you to him."

Valerie jumped down from her bench, and a dozen people fell in after her as she followed Jacob down the hall.

He stopped in front of one of the rooms. The door stood open, but the fluorescent light inside wasn't on. "This is Snowdrop."

Valerie peered into the gloom and could just make out a hunched human figure. "Snowdrop? Is that you?"

No one answered her. She turned around. "I can't see a thing in there."

Jacob crossed the hall to a panel on the wall and threw a switch. The siren went off again. The inmates looked up at the ceiling and all around them, but no one moved a muscle. Valerie turned back to the room and saw that the light was on.

An ancient man sat on the cot with his milky white eyes fixed on the floor in front of him. Valerie moved into the room. "Mr. Cornell? Ebert Cornell?"

The man's head creaked on his neck when he looked up. "Who's there?"

Valerie squatted down in front of him. "I'm Valerie Inglewood, from the Strikeforce Investigation Team. Colonel Tomlinson sent me here to bring you home."

He stared into space, but he couldn't see her. "What's that? Colonel Tomlinson...."

"That's right, Mr. Cornell," Valerie replied. "Your assignment here is finished. You can come back to Strikeforce now."

He blinked, and his old eyes brimmed over with tears. "I can leave now?"

Valerie fought back her own tears.

What this poor man must have endured in this place, all these years! "That's right, Mr. Cornell. We're here to take you home. You're free."

He tottered to his feet, but he stumbled and collapsed against her. Valerie hooked her arm around his ribs and Jacob propped him up on the other side. Between the two of them, they helped him down the hall to the main entrance. The thump of choppers sounded overhead.

The crowd thinned out. Valerie and Jacob helped Ebert Cornell into the first chopper. A long plume of dust obscured the road out of the valley from the cars driving away from EdenCloud. The second chopper took custody of AngelPie and Sri Danke, and Dan Henderson arranged to transport his father's body back to Phoenix.

He stood next to his car and took Valerie's hand. "Will I ever see you again?"

Valerie smiled and blushed. "I'm sure you will. I don't see how we could live the rest of our lives without seeing each other again. I feel like I've known you for years."

"You won't forget me, will you?" he asked. "Tell me our time together here wasn't just some wild one night stand."

"No way," she exclaimed. "I've got your address and phone number and email address. I'm coming to Phoenix to track you down just as soon as we get debriefed by Colonel Tomlinson."

He nodded. "I'm coming to Denver, too. I'm meeting Colonel Tomlinson to get my father's records. Maybe I'll see you there."

"Don't you dare come to Denver without looking me up," Valerie shot back. "If I find out you did, I'll track you down and wring your neck."

He bent over her and kissed her. "I love it when you talk dirty."

She threw her arms around his neck and savored his kiss.

"Behave yourself. Don't forget I can look you up any time and find out if you're not wearing your seat belt."

"Oh, Officer!" he whined. "Handcuff me to the bedpost and spank me. I've been ever so bad!"

Valerie laughed, but she wasn't laughing a few minutes later when she waved to his car disappearing up the road. Every man she ever cared for had a way of disappearing out of her life. The moment she connected with someone, circumstances dragged them away from her. When would it ever change? Was this the price of her place on the Strikeforce Team?

That and a dozen other doubts and fears rolled into her mind and then rolled out of it. Valerie turned back to dealing with business.

She got so swept up in the business of filing their case paperwork and meeting with Colonel Tomlinson for their debrief. She was so busy that she didn't even think about Dan Henderson until a week later.

She pushed her chair back from the table in the commissary in the Strikeforce office building and touched the clean white napkin to the corners of her mouth with a satisfied sigh.

Charlene appeared on the other side of the table and dropped a heavy manila folder onto the table with a loud slap. "Are you finished here?"

Valerie leaned back and patted her stomach. "You don't know how good it is to eat real food again."

Charlene snorted. "You never ate un-real food. As far as I know, you never let a morsel of food pass your lips up at EdenCloud except what you brought there yourself. You were only there for thirty-six hours. You weren't exactly starved."

"It's the thought that counts," Valerie replied. "I have to appreciate good food while I can. I never know when you're going to drag me off to some dungeon where I'll have to survive on bread and water."

"Well, if you're quite finished stuffing your face, get your badge and your weapon and come with me." Charlene waved the folder in her face. "We don't have much time."

Valerie stood up. "What is it now? Not another case, I hope."

"It's not a case," Charlene replied. "We're on our way down to the rifle range. There's a new batch of applicants trying out for a place on the Strikeforce Team, and your old friend Jeff Everson is leading the pack."

The End

92

Don't miss Valerie's next case, in "Bad Blood" – you'll find a taste of that book just after the 'About the Author' section!

About the Author

T.K. Wilde is a long term writer, who writes both fiction and non-fiction, under a number of pen names.

A particular fondness for mysteries, action, and non-standard female characters resulted in this series – we hope you enjoy it!

Books in the Valerie Inglewood Series

The series, in reading order, is

1. Bad Moon Rising

2. One Bad Apple

3. Bad Blood

4. Bad Intent

5. From Bad to Worse

Here is your preview of Book 3 in the series

STRIKEFORCE AGENT

VALERIE INGLEWOOD

BAD BLOOD

T.K. WILDE

Chapter 1

Machine gun fire spattered the side of the building and shattered the bricks. A handful of bullets crashed through the plate glass window. Shards of broken glass rained down on Valerie's head. She kept her eyes closed until the tinkling stopped and the gunfire moved away around the corner.

Valerie raised her head and looked around. Plates of food sat overturned on the floor, and broken plates and soggy napkins littered the place. A few minutes before, Valerie had been sitting down to a hearty breakfast with her partner, Charlene Brockworth, to celebrate the newest member of the Strikeforce Team.

Jeff Everson had earned his place, with a special commendation from Colonel Tomlinson, and now he and his partner, Tiko Bennetta, were assigned to work with Valerie and Charlene on the Denver mob war.

But their celebratory breakfast had just come to an abrupt halt, as gunfire tore the cafe apart, and everyone in the place scattered for cover. Valerie aimed her service pistol at the empty hole where the front window used to be, but the shooter was long gone.

Charlene's voice rang through the remains of the cafe. "Are you all right, Valerie?"

"I'm fine," Valerie replied. "Are you okay?"

A crash answered her. Charlene stepped out of the shadows with her pistol in her hand. "I've had enough of this gangland stuff. Let's go back to the Mackenzie Lodge. At least it was quiet there."

"It was quiet at EdenCloud, too, and I wouldn't want to go back there. Give me the city any day of the week." Valerie brushed broken glass off her clothes and holstered her weapon. "Did you see anything? Did you get a look at anyone in the car?"

Charlene shook her head.

"No one ever sees anything in drive-bys like this. Even if we'd got a look at the shooters, they would probably have been wearing masks."

A few customers poked their heads out of their hiding places. "Where are the others?"

Before Charlene could answer, another explosion of gunfire broke the stillness. Valerie and Charlene hit the floor, but this time, the spray didn't end and fade away. It grew louder and more menacing. Valerie crawled under the nearest table and drew her weapon again.

A moment later, a pair of legs kicked the door open. Valerie caught sight of a man's figure, cradling a machine gun in his hands, but she couldn't see his face. He leveled his gun and let loose another deadly barrage of bullets. They splintered the wooden table over Valerie's head, and she scuttled for cover.

The only place she could find to hide was the waiter's station, and she crawled behind it.

The heavy plywood counter protected her from the bullets, but she couldn't see anything back there. She took one peek around the corner and saw the strange legs walking in her direction.

All of a sudden, a hand closed around her arm. She nearly jumped out of her skin, but, when she turned to look behind her, she found herself nose to nose with Jeff Everson. "Valerie! I've been looking everywhere for you." Jeff whispered against her ear.

"What are you doing back here, Jeff?" she asked, also whispering.

"The same thing you're doing here," he replied. "I'm saving my bacon. I don't care if I'm a federal agent now. I'm not going out there to face a man with a machine gun when I've only got a .44 to defend myself with."

Valerie snickered. "Don't worry. We're all doing the same thing. Nobody wants to lose their life playing the hero. It wouldn't do any good anyway." The machine gun farted again, and Jeff and Valerie huddled close behind the counter. "What the devil is going on out there? He's already destroyed the place. Why doesn't he leave?"

Bullets rattling against the walls interrupted their conversation. In the din of splintering sheetrock and crashing crockery, Jeff leaned over and kissed her. Valerie pulled back in surprise. "What was that for?"

He grinned.

"Just saying hello. We haven't had a moment together since I joined the Strikeforce Team."

He tried to kiss her again, but she shoved him back. "What are you trying to do? We're in the middle of a shoot-out."

"What better time?" he asked. "No one will see us. Your partner is across the room and...." He glanced around. "I don't see my partner anywhere. No one will know."

He kissed her, and the fire of desire blocked out everything else. Valerie let her mouth fall open, and his sweet saliva prickled her tongue. When would they find a moment to go off alone together? He would move into the Strikeforce penthouse any day now. What would happen to their relationship then?

The bullets stopped flying, and the silence brought Valerie back to the present. She pushed him away again, but without much conviction. "We'd better not. We're supposed to be on the job."

He moved away, but his eyes didn't leave her face. "Just remember I'm coming for you."

"I can't wait." Valerie cocked her ears at the sound of footsteps crunching through the broken glass. They came close to the waiters' station, but then they passed on. The shooter sure was taking his time about destroying the place. Wasn't he worried about someone recognizing him?

She glanced over at Jeff. To her horror, he rose up on his knees and peeked over the counter at the shooter. The man turned, and sprayed the back wall with bullets. Jeff dropped down to the floor next to her again. Valerie grabbed his arm.

"What do you think you're doing? Are you trying to get your head shot off?"

"I had to see who it was," he replied. "If there was any chance of identifying him, I had to take the chance."

Valerie hauled him down to the floor. "Don't you ever try anything like that again."

"Don't worry," he replied. "I didn't get shot."

"So did you get a look at him?" she asked.

Jeff shook his head. "Charlene was right. He's wearing a mask."

Another volley of bullets broke off their conversation, but when the cafe fell silent again, a sinking feeling told Valerie the attack was over. The shooter's footsteps crunched through the glass on his way back toward the door. Then he disappeared outside.

No one moved a muscle or made a peep. Charlene didn't call out again or stand up. Valerie and Jeff stayed behind the counter for what seemed like a long time. In the end, Jeff got up on his hands and knees. "It's safe now. He's gone."

They got to their feet. Charlene emerged from a pile of overturned tables on the other side of the café, surveyed the room and stuck her pistol into the holster at her back. She met Valerie and Jeff at the waiters' station. "Well, this place is a write-off. I hope their insurance is up to date."

"I don't think most business insurance policies cover shoot-'em-ups," Jeff remarked.

Valerie put her weapon away. "They can list it under 'Acts of God'."

"This was no act of God." Charlene took out her phone. "Good morning, Colonel Tomlinson. Yes, Sir. That's why I'm calling. We just had another shoot-out here at the Morning Maven Cafe. Yep. Will do." She hung up. "He's assigning us to investigate. I thought he might. Where's Tiko?"

Tiko Bennetta stuck his head with his slicked-back hair out from behind the kitchen door. "I'm in here. We got a situation."

"What's going on?" Charlene asked.

"This wasn't your typical gangland shoot-out," Tiko replied. "This was a premeditated murder. Come have a look."

They followed him through the kitchen to the back office, where the manager sat at his desk with the ballpoint pen hanging from his fingers. His head hung down onto his chest and his mouth dropped open. No one would ever have guessed he hadn't fallen asleep at his desk. Only the black stain spreading over the back of his shirt gave mute testimony that he wouldn't wake up again.

Tiko pointed to the torn cloth of the victim's T-shirt. "Four bullets to the back and they weren't machine gun bullets, either. That shoot-up out front was just a distraction. The killer must have snuck in through the back door, shot Tony, and then beat it while the rest of us were cowering in fear."

Charlene got on her phone again. "Hey, Mort. It's Charlene Brockworth here. Yeah, we've got a stiff for you at 275 Ironwood Street. The Morning Maven Cafe, in the manager's office. Great. See you then." She hung up again. "The Crime Lab is on the way."

Valerie bent over the manager. "What do you know about the vic, Tiko?"

"Tony?" Tiko asked. "Everybody knows Tony Eno. He's a legend in this town."

"Then how come I never heard of him?" Charlene asked.

"Because you're not Italian," Tiko replied.

"Neither are you," Charlene shot back. "Now stop playing games and tell us what you know about him. I guess he was more than just the manager of a coffee shop, or the gangsters wouldn't have made such an effort to kill him."

"You're right, he was a lot more than a manager," Tiko replied. "He was the son of Edith Skipperingham. That's how he got this position in the first place."

"Edith Skipperingham?" Charlene exclaimed. "But she's Frank Lukeman's wife."

"*Ex*-wife," Tiko corrected her. "They split up, and she got bigger than he ever was. It looks like she took half his money and set herself up in business to compete with him. They've been at each other's throats ever since."

"If that's true," Valerie pointed out, "then this Tony Eno would be Frank's son, too. He wouldn't kill his own son to get back at Edith."

Tiko shook his head, but his black eyes twinkled. "Wrong again, Virginia. Tony is Edith's son by another man. Some people say she cheated on Frank and got pregnant while they were still married. Other people think she got pregnant before she got together with Frank. Either way, one thing is certain."

"Enlighten us, O Master," Charlene said, grinning at Tiko.

Tiko puffed himself up. "His father is Danny Seagall."

A hush fell over the group. Jeff looked around. "Did I miss something?"

Valerie sighed. "You just started with the Strikeforce Team, so you don't know. If you'd been around Denver very long, you would know that Danny Seagall is Frank Lukeman's worst enemy. They've been warring for twenty years."

Tiko interrupted. "And now you know why."

"So Frank Lukeman killed Danny and Edith's son," Jeff replied. "That makes the case pretty straightforward."

"Not exactly," Valerie replied. "Frank might have ordered this hit, but he wouldn't pull the trigger himself. He would have sent one of his boys to do the job. Anyway, it's our job to collect the evidence and prove that he did order the hit. It could have been someone else."

"Like who?" Tiko asked. "Tony had a thousand friends and no enemies that I know of. If Frank didn't kill him, I don't know who did."

At that moment, a woman's scream ripped through the cafe. The four investigators went back out to the waiters' station. A man with sweat streaming down his face met them at the door. He grabbed Charlene's hand and pulled her across the room. "He's over here. Quick! You have to call the police. You can still save him."

They followed him across the room. Behind a cluster of overturned tables, a woman knelt by another man, who was lying still and stiff on the floor.

The first thing Valerie noticed was his suit. He wore an immaculate, pinstriped Armani suit and polished leather brogues. Who dressed like that to come down to their corner coffee shop for breakfast?

Blood stained the dead man's crisp white shirt, and bullet holes marred his jacket. The woman pressed his hand to her heart and sobbed. The first man tugged at Charlene's hand. "Quick! Call the police!"

Charlene sighed. "We are the police. Whoever did this, we're the ones who will investigate."

"But you can save him," the man insisted. "Call the paramedics. They can hook him up to their machines and save him."

Charlene gazed down at the motionless form. In front of their eyes, a pool of blood spread out on the floor under the victim's back. "I'm afraid no one can save him now. The Crime Lab will be here soon, and after that, the Coroner will take your friend's body."

"He's not my friend," the man told her. "He's my brother."

Charlene's head came up in a hurry. "Your brother?"

The man nodded. "He came into town for business and we met here for breakfast. We don't go out very often, but we decided to make this a special occasion. Then *this* had to happen."

"Look, Mister.... What did you say your name was?" Charlene asked.

"I'm Tom Duvall, and this is my wife Margaret," he replied. "My brother was Tim Duvall."

"I'm very sorry for your loss, Mr. Duvall," Charlene replied, "but your brother is the unfortunate victim of some very nasty mob activity that's been plaguing the area for some time. We've been trying to break it up, and this was just another battle in a very long war. I'm afraid your brother got caught in the crossfire."

Tom looked around the battered cafe in desperation. "But that's impossible. This is Denver, the Mile-High City. There's no mob activity here. I've lived here for forty years, and nothing like this ever happened before."

Charlene's shoulders sagged.

"I know it's hard to believe, but the mob elements in this war have kept their activities under cover for a long time. They only started breaking out onto the streets about a year ago. That's when we got called in."

Tom stared down at his brother.

"This can't be happening."

"I'm so sorry." Charlene waved toward the door. "Let's get you two out of here. You'll feel better in the open air."

Tom shook his head. "I can't leave him."

Valerie studied the dead man. He didn't come to Denver to transact business in a suit like that – not any legal kind of business, anyway. Charlene escorted Tom out of the cafe, but Valerie couldn't tear herself away from this second victim. Jeff appeared at her side.

"The Crime Lab is here. We have to go."

Valerie nodded and bent over Margaret. She still bathed the victim's pale hand with her tears.

"Come on, Mrs. Duvall. We have to leave now to let the Crime Lab people work."

They met Tom and Charlene on the street outside, just as the Crime Lab techs pulled up in their unmarked white van.

"There's one victim in the front under the tables and another one in the manager's office."

Tom looked around, but it was obvious that he didn't see anything in front of him. Margaret wept silent tears and held Valerie's hand in a death grip. Valerie nodded toward Charlene's car a few parking spaces away. "We'd better take them home. They can't go alone."

Charlene nodded and they steered the bereaved couple towards the car. Valerie glanced over her shoulder and spotted Jeff staring at her. At the same moment, Tiko came out of the cafe and said something to Jeff. He waved his arms, and his cheeks flushed with excitement. Jeff turned away, and the two men crossed the street to their own car.

Where were they going? When would Valerie see Jeff again? He'd been too busy with his initiation procedures and assignments to spend much time in the office. And Valerie was busy with the organized crime training she needed to complete before Colonel Tomlinson would assign her to the Denver mob war.

Of course, Charlene had kept their observation of Jeff's try-out for the Strikeforce Team a secret.

He never knew that Valerie was watching him on the rifle range and the obstacle course. And she'd never been near enough to tell him – until just now behind the cafe counter, with bullets flying. Leave it to him to take that opportunity to kiss her.

Find out what happens next-

Make sure to get your copy as soon as its released !

MIXING FAMILY FEUDS, MURDER
AND MOB WARFARE IS A BAD IDEA....
BAD
BLOOD
STRIKEFORCE AGENT
VALERIE INGLEWOOD
T.K. WILDE

Other Books from Dreamstone Publishing

Dreamstone publishes books in a wide variety of categories – here are some of our other bestselling non fiction books:-

Moving Beyond the Unspoken Grief:
A doctor's memoir of her own IVF
journey as a patient
By Dr Sarah Lnyy

Should I Quit?
Resilience for a turbulent world
By Mike Gordon

"Icebreakers : How to Empower,
Motivate and Inspire Your Team,
Through Step-by-Step Activities That
Boost Confidence, Resilience and
Create Happier Individuals"
By Di McMath

All Books available from all Amazon sites and other book stores, and available for Kindle too!

And here are some of our bestselling romance books from Arietta Richmond.

Be first to know when our next books are coming out – sign up for our newsletter at

http://www.dreamstonepublishing.com